DOCTOR IN LOVE

In this hilarious romantic comedy, Richard Gordon awakes one morning with a headache. It takes him a while to realize he is ill – after all he is a doctor! Dr Pennyworth diagnoses jaundice and prescribes a spell in hospital, and amongst the bedpans and injections on Honesty Ward, Richard falls in love – with his very own Florence Nightingale. When he learns he has a rival for her affections, unwilling to lose his love to the pachyderm Dr Hinxman, Richard sets out to impress...

DOCTOR IN LOVE

DOCTOR IN LOVE

by

Richard Gordon

Dales Large Print Books
Long Preston, North Yorkshire,
BD23 4ND, England.

British Library Cataloguing in Publication Data.

Gordon, Richard
    Doctor in love.

        A catalogue record of this book is
        available from the British Library

        ISBN   1-84262-251-X pbk

Dales Large Print is an imprint of Library Magna Books Ltd.

Printed and bound in Great Britain by
T.J. (International) Ltd., Cornwall, PL28 8RW

To
ANTHONY & SIMON
naturally

1

It is a fact well known to the medical profession that doctors marry either nurses, other doctors, or barmaids. During the most marriageable years these are the only women they meet. Indeed, at the age when other young men's fancies first lightly turn to thoughts of matrimony they are unable to marry at all, being still supported by an allowance from home. It is small consolation to reflect that the further you ascend the evolutionary scale the longer you find the young depend on the parent, which makes medical students the highest form of animal life known to science.

Although my classmates at St Swithin's Hospital included a couple of harassed young men who arrived at lectures with notebooks dutifully sharing string bags with sprouts and soap-flakes, a married medical student is almost as much an impossibility as a married Boy Scout. Then the magic touch of a diploma changes his emotional life as violently as his economic one. As an unqualified scallywag he has the alternative of dishonourable intentions or no intentions at all; but after the examination results engagement rings sparkle round the nurses' home as gaily as summer stars, and if the Royal Colleges of Physicians and Surgeons knew how many unions were first solemnized by their examiners they would be much alarmed.

The first of my companions to wed was Tony Benskin, who married a night nurse. This was reasonable, as he had once offered matrimony to all of them on duty one night to invalidate an over-enthusiastic proposal to one earlier in the evening. It was almost two years until I saw him again, for medical students at the end of their course, like ships' passengers at the end of their voyage, exchange addresses with more enthusiasm than earnestness. I ran into him one summer evening in the corridors of St Swithin's, where I was still working on the junior resident staff.

'Tony!' I cried. I stared at him in alarm. His face was pale and unshaven, his eye wild and bloodshot, his hair and his tie awry. 'Tony! What on earth's the matter?'

'Hello, Richard,' he said absently. 'I brought Molly into the hospital last night.'

'Oh, my dear fellow! Was it an accident?'

'Of course it wasn't an accident! We planned it.'

'You mean... Oh, I see. She's having a baby?'

'What, you mean you didn't know?' His tone indicated an affair of universal importance.

'No, I'm afraid the news didn't reach me. So she's in the tender care of the midder department? There's nothing to worry about.'

'Nothing to worry about! What do you understand about it? You've never had a baby.'

'But it was a normal pregnancy, I hope?'

'Oh, yes, her pregnancy was normal enough, down to the last molecule of haemoglobin. But just think of the things which might go wrong now! Why, at the best it may be a breech. It could be a persistent occipito-postenor or a transverse lie, or a placenta praevia or a prolapsed cord. She might have a PPH or a Caesar or anything... Do you remember all those frightful pictures in the midder books?' He thrust his hands disconsolately into his trouser pockets. 'It's alarming, isn't it?'

Seeing that his clinical detachment was as disarranged as his appearance, I laid a hand

13

consolingly on his shoulder.

'Remember all the women who're having babies every minute of the day. Why, at this very moment Molly will be lying there pleasantly doped with pethidine, listening to old Sister Studholme telling her to bear down nicely, dear, and try and save your pains.'

'But that's the ruddy trouble!' Tony looked more anxious than ever. 'I rushed her in all the way from Hampstead in the middle of the night, and not a thing's happened since.'

'She's just gone off the boil, as they say in the midwifery trade.'

'But think what it *might* be! She could have uterine inertia, deep transverse arrest, contracted pelvis...'

'Look,' I decided. 'What you need is a drink.'

He paused. 'You know, Richard, I believe you're absolutely right.'

He calmed a little under the effect of three large whiskies in the King George opposite the Hospital.

'I'm afraid I'm not quite myself,' he apologized.

'But that's understandable in the circumstances. Traditional, in fact.'

'I'm sorry, Richard. I ought to have slapped you on the back and asked you how

14

you were and talked about the good old days, and so on. But it's upsetting all this – bringing new life into the world, and so on.'

I laughed. 'I'm not sure they shouldn't have stuck you in the labour ward instead of Molly.'

'It may look funny to you, but it's a shattering prospect for the first time. Just wait till it's your turn.'

'Not me! I'm going to stay a bachelor. Changing imperceptibly from gay young to dirty old.'

'Bet you fifty quid you don't!'

I considered the proposition. 'I'll take you on. It's a good bet, because I'm determined to get my FRCS before I even think of marrying.' I still wanted to specialize in surgery, and the Fellowship of the Royal College was as essential as a flying licence to a prospective pilot. 'And at the present rate I can't see much chance of passing the exam before I get prostatic hypertrophy and the male menopause.'

'But you'll *have* to get married, old man. Take it from me, a doctor's got to. The patients don't like you messing about with their wives unless they know you've got one of your own at home. Then you must have someone to answer the telephone and open the door and keep all the NHS cards straight and cook the dinner and do the laundry.'

'I could get a housekeeper.'

'The only housekeeper you could possibly employ would have to be so ugly and respectable she wouldn't bear living with. No, Richard. You'll have to settle for the pipe and armchair and the slippers and taking the dog for a walk at closing time.'

I took a mouthful of beer thoughtfully.

'But even allowing you're right, Tony – where do I find the right girl? Supposing I picked the wrong one?'

'Sheer defeatism! Anyway, what's the matter with one of the matron's little charges? They're all healthy girls, they know how to cook and make the beds, and they're trained to put up with any amount of irritation from crotchety old men. You couldn't ask for more. It has long been my contention that the most useful function of any nursing school in the country is turning out a supply of fully trained doctors' wives. Though,' he added reflectively, 'they tend to worry a lot about the regularity of your bowels.' Suddenly I noticed his jaw drop. 'It's just occurred to me,' he muttered. 'Supposing the poor little thing's got mixed-up guts or no feet or two heads, or any of those hundreds of congenital defects we had to learn about in embryology?'

'Don't be ridiculous, Tony! Despite the fact that it has you for a father, it will turn out a perfectly healthy and normal baby. The very worst you can worry about is twins.'

He shook his head. 'At least it can't be that – I sent Molly down to the X-ray department long ago. Do you want to see baby's first photo? I've got it in the back of the car.'

The next afternoon I was surprised to see Molly Benskin sitting in the sunshine that pierced the dusty plane trees in the hospital courtyard, still looking like an overripe poppy-head.

'Hello!' I said. 'I thought you'd be otherwise engaged.'

She wrinkled her snub nose. 'It's all Tony's fault. Instead of acting in a perfectly calm and professional manner as he would if I was his patient instead of his wife–'

'He's been behaving like any other expectant father?'

'Oh, much worse! Do you know, for the last month he's been trying to take my blood pressure pretty well hourly? And every time I had a backache he got the car out. In the end I couldn't stop him rushing me here at four in the morning as though I was on fire. I think he was scared stiff he'd have to deliver it himself.'

'As far as I remember, Tony was never very accurate at midder,' I told her sympathetically. 'When I was a student with him we always seemed to arrive either three hours too early or five minutes too late.'

'Now I've got to stay in the ward, I haven't got any of my things, my hair's terrible, I look most unglamorous, the food's uneatable, sister's a bitch, and I'm fed up.' She pouted. 'On top of that, I feel that I'm never going to have the poor little thing at all.'

'Don't you worry, Molly. So do all expectant mothers. It's never been known to fail yet.'

Two days afterwards she was delivered of an eight-pound baby boy, which Tony Benskin later carried through the main gate of the hospital with the expression of one who had discovered and patented the process himself. Helping them into the car, I was surprised to find that even I experienced strong avuncular feelings. Marriage, I had always felt, was some sort of disease which creeps up on everyone with age, like hardening of the arteries. For the first time I began to wonder how long my immunity would last.

2

The following morning I woke in my bare room in the St Swithin's resident staff quarters feeling like Sisera, who I remembered learning in Divinity had a tent-peg driven through his temple while he slept. The old diagnosis would have been *hangover vulgaris*; but now that my former classmates were scattering both geographically and professionally I rarely had anyone to go drinking with, and I had gone to bed at eleven after a cup of coffee with the night nurse down in casualty.

In the gloomy residents' dining-room, sitting beneath the chiding eyes of Hippocrates, Lord Lister, and Sir William Osler, I found that I couldn't eat my breakfast. This was unusual, because after even our most shameful student debauches I was always ready for my porridge and kippers as usual the next morning. I managed to swallow a cup of tea, then put on my white coat and crossed the hospital courtyard to my laboratory.

At the time I was coming to the end of my

appointment as the junior resident pathologist I spent my days in the pathology block, sitting at a bench richly engrained with the brilliant blues, greens, and reds used for staining bacteria, doing calculations and tests on 'specimens'. These were of various sorts, and either sent across daily from the wards by the trayful or borne to us proudly by out-patients in a selection of jamjars and beer bottles produced from inside the jacket or shopping basket.

'Do you mind if we have the window closed?' I asked the junior pathology demonstrator, my overseer. I pulled a high wooden laboratory stool to my usual place. 'It's a bit nippy this morning.'

'Nippy? It's a lovely hot summer's day!'

I drew my microscope towards me and shivered.

'Be a good lad and get on with this pile of blood counts,' he continued. 'There's been a rush of them over from the wards. Then there's some urines over there I'd like you to tackle when you're free. They're beginning to niff a bit.'

When the demonstrator went off to lecture I shut all the windows. Then I was surprised to find that the weather had suddenly turned warmer and I was sweating. The climate was particularly irritating, because that morning my work was twice as troublesome as usual. I had difficulty in focusing the microscope, I kept shaking drops of blood from the little glass sides, and I couldn't add up. By lunch time I slunk back to my room and laid down, wondering why I felt so tired.

It didn't occur to me that I was ill. It never does to doctors, who are as shocked to find themselves sick as a policeman to discover that his home has been burgled or a fireman to see his own roof on fire. It was almost through curiosity that I rummaged for a clinical thermometer I kept somewhere in my sock drawer, and slipped it under my tongue.

'Good God!' I said. I had a temperature of a hundred and three.

I sat down on the edge of my bed, faced with the unnerving problem of self-diagnosis.

I gingerly felt my pulse. Ninety-six. Crossing to the mirror I stuck out my tongue, which looked like the inside of an old kettle. I stared down my throat, but found I couldn't see very far. Opening my shirt, I ran a stethoscope over as much of my chest as possible, and discovered that listening to your own breath-sounds for the first time is as alarming as hearing a record of your own voice. After thinking for a few minutes I decided that it must be typhoid fever.

Another characteristic of doctors is never allowing themselves to be ill by half-measures. In the process of self-diagnosis they think first of all the fatal diseases, next of the most outlandish, thirdly of the most uncomfortable, and finally reach a decision which would have had them thrown out of any qualifying examination in the country. Failing typhoid, I suspected glanders, psittacosis, or incipient cholera, and remembering the light-hearted way in which we manipulated dangerous bacteria in the laboratory I threw in rabies and plague as well.

After diagnosis comes treatment, and fumbling in my shaving locker for some white tablets which I thought were aspirins I swallowed a few. A further peculiarity of the physician healing himself is a wild disregard for labels and dosage: men who terrify patients by repeating sternly 'Not more than two teaspoonsful after food' treat their own complaints largely with the pharmaceutical samples sent from drug manufacturers, in doses of either a moderate handful or a large swig. Feeling afterwards that I should call for professional advice, I picked up my bedside telephone and rang my friend Grimsdyke, who was working as a resident anaesthetist in the operating theatre.

'I'm ill,' I told him, describing my symptoms. 'What do you think I should do?'

'Go and see a doctor.'

'Look here, this isn't a laughing matter. I feel terrible.'

'Seriously, old lad. Get one of the house physicians. I don't know much more about pure medicine than I do about pure mathematics. We live in an age of specialization, don't we? Must get back to the theatre now– Patient looks a bit blue.'

I then rang Hinxman, houseman to Dr Pennyworth, the St Swithin's senior physician.

'You've probably got the measles,' he said cheerfully on the other end of the line. 'There's a lot of it about at the moment.'

'I've had it. A most nasty attack when I was six.'

'It's quite possible to get it twice, of course. And it's usually much worse the second time. Or it might be mumps. You know what that leads to, don't you?' He roared with laughter: fellow-doctors show as little sympathy for each other in trouble as fellow-golfers. 'It's a bit of a nuisance, because we've hardly got a spare bed in the

23

ward. But I'll pop along and see you when I've got a moment.'

Hinxman appeared an hour or so later. He was a red-faced, curly-headed young man much given to tweeds and pipes, who always entered a room as though coming from a brisk tramp across open moors on a gusty day. I found his aggressive healthiness deeply depressing as I nervously watched his broad pink hands pummel my abdomen.

'Deep breath, old man,' he commanded. He frowned.

For the first time I realized how alarming a doctor sounds when he goes 'M'm'.

'Think I can get a touch of the spleen there,' he added.

'Good Lord!' I jumped up. 'It might be one of those horrible leukaemias.'

'Yes, and it may be the chlorotic anaemia of young virgins. Don't get excited about it. I haven't felt a spleen for weeks, anyway, and I'm probably wrong. I'll get old Pennyboy along when he looks into the hospital at six. Meanwhile, go to bed.'

'Bed?' I protested. 'But I don't really want to go to bed. I hate lying down doing nothing.'

'My dear chap, you must. The first thing any physician does is to put his victim to

24

bed and tell him to keep quiet. It doesn't do the patient the slightest harm, and it gives everyone time to think. Why, we've had some of our patients in bed for weeks upstairs while we've been thinking. We're not like surgeons, you know – never happy unless they're doing something violent.'

Dr Pennyworth himself came to my room that evening, followed by Hinxman and his medical registrar. The hospital's senior physician was a small, thin, pale man with two tufts of grey hair jutting over his ears, dressed in a black jacket and pin-striped trousers. He was so quiet and so modest that he seemed to enter the room like a ghost, without using the door. He stood by my bedside, softly wished me good evening, perched a pair of rimless pince-nez on his nose, and inspected me through them in silence.

'Ever been in India?' he asked mysteriously.

'No, sir.'

'H'm.'

After some moments' thought he gently took my hand and stood staring at my nails. This I recognized as the manner of a true physician: a surgeon would have burst into the room, pummelled me briskly, exclaimed 'Does it hurt? Where? There? Don't worry, old fellow, we'll have it out!' and telephoned the operating theatre. Dr Pennyworth silently listened to my chest, scratched the soles of my feet, pulled down an eyelid, shook me by the hand, and after a whispered discussion with his assistants disappeared as softly as he came.

As no one had told me what was wrong, I lay staring at the ceiling and speculating on the further possibility of malaria, cerebral abscess, and *spirochoetsis ictero-haemorrhagic.* I had almost given myself up for lost by the time Hinxman reappeared.

'You're to be warded, old man,' he announced cheerfully. 'I've fixed everything up. Just slip on a dressing-gown and wander up to Honesty when you feel like it. Try not to breathe on too many people on the way, won't you?'

'But what have I got?'

'Oh, didn't we tell you? Look at your eyeballs.'

'Good lord!' I exclaimed, turning to the mirror. 'Jaundice.'

'Yes, you'd pass for a good-looking Chinaman anywhere. I'll come and see you later. By the way, we'll be needing a contribution for your own laboratory.'

Collecting my toothbrush, I obediently left the residency for the main hospital block and made my way upstairs to Honesty Ward. I had rarely been ill before, and I had never been in a ward in a subjective capacity at all. I now approached the experience with the feeling of a judge mounting the steps to his own dock.

'Well, well, fancy seeing you,' said the staff nurse, a motherly blonde I had once met at a hospital dance. 'Sister's off, so I've put you in the corner. You're not terribly infectious, and we'll have you on barrier nursing.'

I got into the white iron bed, which was ready with hot-water bottle in knitted cover, red rubber sheet next to the mattress, backrest, air-ring, and a small enamel bowl on the locker in case I wanted to put my teeth in it.

'Sorry we can't have you in a side-room,' she apologized. 'But they're both in use. One might be free in a few days,' she added significantly, 'and you can move in then.'

My first few days as a patient were delightful. My disease wasn't serious – though I kept remembering the nasty phrase in one of my textbooks, 'a small percentage of cases are fatal' – and it had the advantage that no treatment whatever was known to medical science. This left my days and nights undisturbed by having to swallow oversized pills or having to tolerate over-used needles. All I had to do was lie on my back and get better.

But I soon realized that being ill in a modern hospital is far from a passive process. A few years ago it dawned on physicians that patients shouldn't be allowed simply to rot in bed, but should be provided with daily exercise for both body and mind. This idea is now applied so enthusiastically and ward routine has become so strenuous that only people of a basically sound constitution can stand it.

Our day, like the Army's, started at six-thirty with a wash in tepid water, and continued almost without a break until lights-out at nine. Apart from the regular upheavals caused by bed making, meals, hot drinks, blanket baths, temperature-taking, visits by the doctors, and the distribution of 'bottles', there always seemed to be some hospital functionary waiting to see you. Each morning there appeared a blonde girl looking like a Wimbledon champion in a white overall, who came from the Physiotherapy Department to conduct a horizontal PT class. When we had flexed our knees and twiddled our toes in unison under the bedclothes, another girl arrived from the Occupational Therapy Unit with a basket of felt scraps for making pink bunnies. Afterwards came the hospital librarian to see if you felt like reading, the hospital dietitian to see if you felt like eating, and the hospital chaplain to see if you felt like death. Next appeared the man who brought the post, the boy who sold the newspapers, and several women with brooms who swept under the beds and carried on a loud conversation between themselves about everyone's illnesses. If you still had time, you could explore the arid stretches of the morning and afternoon radio programmes through the headphones, or swap symptoms with your neighbour. There was a welcome period of enforced sleep after lunch, but this was generally disturbed by fifty students clattering in for a ward-round or one of the medical staff appearing to examine you to test some private theory. Later, those of us allowed up sat round the empty fireplace stroking the ward cat, smoking our pipes, and exchanging opinions in a tranquilly companionable atmosphere reminiscent of an old men's home.

It was in these circumstances that I first fell seriously in love.

3

She was the new night nurse on Honesty Ward. She was a pretty, pale girl, with large dark eyes and thick curly hair on which her official cap perched ridiculously, like the top of a *vol-au-vent*. She had a playful way of looking at you when she spoke, and the first words she addressed to me – 'Would you like Horlicks or Ovaltine?' – sent odd sensations running up my spinal cord.

I had then been in the ward five days, the time I later learned from other nurses at which young men confined to bed start becoming amorous. Physicians perhaps overlook that patients' feelings towards sex, like their feelings towards beer and tobacco, are not automatically held in abeyance while enjoying the benefit of medical care in hospital. Seeing the same half a dozen young women regularly all day naturally concentrates the invalid's thoughts on any one of them, which has led many a convalescence to run concurrently with a honeymoon. The patient's state is probably exacerbated by the nursing tradition of twice daily 'doing the backs' – that is, massaging the lower spine with surgical spirit as a precaution against bedsores, which I understand is the method used to encourage recalcitrant bulls in the Argentine.

It was clearly worth making the night nurse's closer acquaintance. As soon as the ward was dark, the flowers had been removed, the day nurses had gratefully reached for their corridor capes, and sister had left for the modest evening pleasures of the sisters' home, I felt for the dressing-gown in my locker and crept out of bed.

She was in the small kitchen just outside the ward, starting to butter a large pile of bread for the patients' breakfast.

'Hello,' I said.

She looked up. 'Hello. But shouldn't you be in bed?'

'I just thought I'd like to establish social contact as well as our professional relationship.'

Stretching her apron, she gave me a curtsy. 'I am indeed honoured, kind sir, that a second-year houseman should take such trouble with a second-year nurse. Aren't you terribly infectious?'

'Not much at this stage. Anyway, I'll be

frightfully careful not to touch anything. I'm afraid that I've just forgotten your name, Nurse–?'

'Florence Nightingale.'

I laughed, but catching her eye apologized quickly. 'I'm terribly sorry. Of course, there *could* be a nurse called Florence Nightingale... I mean, really it's quite a common name, though I suppose unusual...'

'Oh, don't worry. I'm quite used to it. My mother was desperately keen on the Red Cross. Hence the name. Hence the career. My friends call me Sally, by the way. But oughtn't you really to stay in the ward?'

'You're not worried about the night sisters, are you? They won't be on the prowl for hours yet.'

'Ah, the night sisters! "How now, you secret, black, and midnight hags! What is't you do? A deed without a name?"'

'You must be the first nurse I've ever heard quote Shakespeare on duty,' I said in surprise.

She went on buttering a piece of bread with a faintly aggressive air. 'You housemen! You seem to think we confine our reading to Evelyn Pearce's textbooks and the Engagement column in the *Telegraph*. Didn't you see me when the Dramatic Society did *As*

You Like It?'

'No, I'm afraid I missed that one,' I confessed. But seeing a common interest in sight I continued warmly, 'I was terribly keen on the Dramatic Society myself. When I was a student and had more time.'

'I know. I saw your last appearance. It was the week I arrived as a new probationer, and I'll never forget it.'

This was perhaps unfortunate. My dramatic career at St Swithin's had reached its climax with the hospital production of *The Middle Watch*, in which I was cast as the Commander. At the start of the second scene the Captain, played by Grimsdyke, was to be discovered alone in his cabin turning over the pages of *The Field*, until interrupted by a knock and the appearance of Tony Benskin as Ah Fong the Chinese servant. Unfortunately I had mistimed the length of the interval, and Tony and I were still drinking pints of beer in the King George when the curtain rose. There being no knock, Grimsdyke anxiously scanned the entire *Field*, throwing imploring glances into the wings. He then thumbed his way through the *Illustrated London News*, the *Tatler*, and the *Sphere*, and finished the *Sketch* and *Punch* before striding off the stage in a fury and bringing down the curtain, leaving the audience mystified for the rest of the evening at the significance of this short but powerful scene.

'Are you sure you're feeling quite well?' Sally Nightingale continued, interrupting her slicing and laying a hand softly on my cheek. 'You certainly *do* seem a little warm.'

I was just reflecting how much pleasanter this was than having a glass-and-mercury icicle tasting of Dettol rammed under your tongue, when the door opened and Hinxman walked in.

'What are you doing here?' he said immediately.

'Oh, hello, old man. Yes, I know I should be in bed by rights. But being in the trade I thought I could take a few liberties with ward routine.'

'Routine? It's nothing whatever to do with routine. It's a matter of your treatment.'

'Have you met our new night nurse?' I asked.

'I know Nurse Nightingale very well. She was on day duty here until last week. Good evening, Sally.'

'Good evening, Roger.'

'Oh, I'm sorry,' I apologized. 'I didn't realize you'd met.'

There was a silence, in which I felt that my professional adviser and colleague was behaving oddly. Hinxman was one of those enviably uncomplicated men who sing in their baths and never have hangovers or catch colds or feel draughts, and he had the most amiable personality in the whole resident staff quarters. We had previously enjoyed a friendship which ran to mutual loans of razor-blades and textbooks, but now he was breathing heavily and staring at me as though I were some particularly striking specimen in a bottle in the pathology museum.

'Well, you're the doctor.' I shrugged my shoulders, remembering that many young housemen appear weighty when first testing the delicate balance of the doctor-patient relationship. I decided to obey graciously, and said lightly to Sally Nightingale: 'Good night, Nurse. I'll get back to my little waterproofed cot. If I'm still awake, come and talk to me when Dr Hinxman's gone.'

The next morning the motherly staff nurse hooked my treatment board to the foot of my bed. 'You're on complete bed rest,' she announced.

'Oh no!'

'Yes, Mr Hinxman's written you up for it.'

'But what on earth for? I'm getting better. Why, I ought to be out of hospital completely in a few days.'

'I really don't know, I'm afraid. Ours is not to reason why, but to do what the houseman tells us.'

My annoyance came less from the prospect of immobility than the threat it held – bedpans. These traditional features of the hospital scene, which defy the laws of geometry by possessing length and breadth but not depth, have never had, nor deserved, a word written in their favour. So far I had escaped them, but from now on I should have to catch the eye of the junior probationer like everyone else. I decided angrily to tackle Hinxman on his line of treatment as soon as he appeared.

'Look here,' I complained. 'I must say, this bed-rest business is about the limit. Why, I'm pretty well convalescent! Or have you just got me muddled up with someone else?'

Hinxman stared at me in silence. His face was pinker than ever; his eyes were heavy and bloodshot; his hands were thrust deep into the pockets of his white coat, among the percussion hammers, tuning-forks, and other little diagnostic toys beloved by physicians.

'You are at liberty to complain to the Chief about my treatment if you want to.'

'Oh, I wouldn't want to go as far as that. After all, we're both in the trade. I know doctors make rotten patients, but I'm prepared to do as I'm told. I just can't see the point of it, that's all.'

Expression for a second played on his face like the top of a milk saucepan caught at the boil. Then he turned and strode down the ward, with the step of a man finding things too much for him.

4

Romances in hospital, like romances at sea, progress rapidly. This is probably because both patients and passengers have little else to occupy their thoughts between meals. I spent the following days lying strictly in bed trying to read Boswell's *Life of Johnson* and thinking about Sally Nightingale, and the nights staying awake trying to snatch brief chats as she passed in the romantic twilight of the sleeping ward. Like the addict waiting for his daily dose of morphine, I found myself fretting as the evening dragged through its routine of supper, bedpans, and thermometers towards eight o'clock, when the tousled day staff went off duty and Sally reappeared in her fresh starched wrappings.

'Would you care for a little barley water?' she asked as she came to my corner a few nights later. 'I've just made some.'

'Barley water? I'd love it, thanks.'

It would have been all the same if she'd offered hemlock.

'And how are you tonight, Richard?'

'Immeasurably better for seeing you.'

'Now, now!' She gave me a playful look. 'Don't you realize you should think of me purely as your nurse?'

'But that's impossible! Do you know, when I got this beastly disease I thought it was about the unluckiest thing that had happened to me for a long time. But the moment you walked into the ward, Sally... Well, I began to feel that it was the brightest event of my life.'

She laughed as she gave my pillow a professional smoothing. 'Pure delirium, doctor.'

'I'm not at all febrile. Just you feel.'

I had often heard the expression about laying cool hands on fevered brows but I had never until then experienced it. It was most satisfying.

'Perhaps for the sake of us both I'd better fetch you an ice-bag.'

Just at this moment I became aware that Hinxman, too, was standing at my bedside.

'Hello,' I said in surprise. 'Rather early with your night round this evening, aren't you?'

He made no reply. Instead, he stared hard and said, 'Nurse Nightingale, I should like the night report, if you please.'

'Of course, Dr Hinxman. If you wish.'

Hinxman listened to the report sitting under the green-shaded lamp at Sister's desk a few feet from my bed, and afterwards he settled there to write up his notes. He was still working when at last I fell asleep. The next morning I found myself prescribed three-hourly injections of Vitamin C and a diet of soya flour soup.

This rivalry naturally acted as a supercharger to my increasingly powerful feelings about Sally Nightingale. To lose her to such a passionless pachyderm as Hinxman struck me as not only a personal tragedy but a shocking waste. But I was miserably conscious of my present disadvantages in wooing her. I was static, and Hinxman was menacingly mobile; and though I was entitled to enjoy her company all night, Hinxman now stood sentry at Sister's desk until I joined in the snores of the rest of the ward.

My one advantage came on Thursday nights, when Dr Pennyworth's firm was on emergency duty and his house physician liable to be called at any time to the casualty room by the main gate. The next Thursday I was delighted to see Hinxman's combination of lights flash in the indicator above the ward telephone, and he had to pay the penalty of choosing a self-sacrificing profession by taking himself downstairs to see a suspected coronary thrombosis.

'What *are* you doing to poor Roger Hinxman?' asked Sally, appearing almost at once from the sluice room.

I felt a little disappointed that she seemed to find such a serious affair amusing.

'What's he doing to *me?*' I replied warmly. 'Why, the fellow's breaking his Hippocratic oath every time he picks up my treatment board – that bit about not administering any noxious thing, and so on.'

She laughed. 'I suppose I should be gratified. But it's a rather unusual way for a girl to be fought over.'

'Is he in love with you?' I asked anxiously.

'Oh, of course. Roger's been in love with me since my first day in hospital. I broke a thermometer and he told Sister he did it. He's really awfully sweet, you know. But he *does* make me feel like a piece of china in a bull shop sometimes.'

This sounded encouraging. Feeling that the coronary in casualty might easily turn out to be a simple case of indigestion, I immediately asked if she'd like to come out to dinner when I was better.

'That's a terribly bad principle,' she replied.
'What is?'

'Going out with your convalescent patients. When you see me in a world full of other women you'll think I'm just like any other banana in the bunch.'

'Not a bit,' I said stoutly. 'I'm absolutely certain you're more beautiful than ever out of uniform.'

'You'll think I look about four feet tall and sixteen years old. It's wonderful how this get-up puts years on you, isn't it? I suppose it's designed to give girls authority to tell men old enough to be their fathers to get back into bed.'

'But uniform suits you wonderfully, too. It makes you look like a sort of clinical Joan of Arc.'

She tucked in my bedclothes. 'I'm afraid the only resemblance is that a lot of people would like to see me burnt alive. I've got to watch my step with matron's office just now. I'm due for my second-year report, and I don't really want to be thrown out.'

I saw Hinxman's silhouette appear beyond the double glass doors of the ward.

'Will you come, Sally?' I whispered. 'I know an awfully cosy little place in Soho.'

'All right,' she whispered back. 'Slip a note

into the nurses' home when you're in circulation.'

Then she laughed and disappeared, to pretend she was fixing an intravenous drip.

Hinxman did nothing to my treatment board that night. But the crisis came three nights later, when he arrived to find Sally carrying out standing instructions for patients on full bed-rest by giving me a blanket bath. The next morning I found myself written up for a turpentine enema.

'It certainly *is* strange treatment,' said Sister, when I complained angrily. 'It's possible Dr Hinxman made a mistake.'

'I'm quite certain he didn't make any mistake at all. And I absolutely and completely refuse to have it, Sister. I'll discharge myself from hospital first.'

'Perhaps you'd better have a word with him yourself,' she suggested tactfully. Like all St Swithin's sisters, she knew much more that went on in the ward than her nurses gave her credit for. 'I'll get him to come over from the residency.'

My interview with Hinxman was fortunately held behind screens, which had been put round my bed in anticipation of his sentence being carried out.

'What's all this damn nonsense about

enemas?' I demanded.

In reply, he clenched and unclenched his fists. 'You rotter,' he said.

'That's a fine way to speak to a colleague, I must say.'

'I love Sally more than anything else in the world.'

'Oh, do you? And so, it happens, do I.'

'I intend to marry her.'

'And so do I.'

It was the first time I had decided on the fact, and I think the answer surprised me as much as him.

He stood breathing heavily. 'I've known her for more than two years.'

'I've known her for less than two weeks. And I've made more progress.'

'Look here, Gordon! I'm not up to all these fancy tricks. I'm no ... blasted Casanova. I'm an ordinary simple chap, and I love her. If you try to ... to...' But words were beyond him. He crashed one fist into another, then silently pushed his way through the screens and disappeared.

'I'm not having the enema,' I called after him. 'I'll complain to Pennyworth tomorrow.'

When Dr Pennyworth reached my bedside on his ward-round the following afternoon Hinxman seemed strangely composed. I supposed that was because he had already countermanded the enema, and thought that I had nothing to complain about.

'How are you getting on?' whispered Dr Pennyworth, peering at me through his pince-nez.

'He's sleeping very badly,' cut in Hinxman, before I could say anything. 'We've tried him on all the usual narcotics of course, sir. But he seems to be one of these resistant cases.'

'Very interesting.'

'So I thought, sir, as he's desperate, you could prescribe him an effective dosage.'

'Sleep,' murmured Dr Pennyworth as I tried to protest, 'is the physician's greatest friend. "Oh Sleep! It is a gentle thing, Beloved from pole to pole?" Eh?' He then prescribed with his own pen a dose of barbiturate that would have kept a woodful of owls quiet.

'You'll have to swallow them all,' said Sister, handing me the scarlet capsules that evening. 'It's Doctor Pennyworth's own orders, you know.'

I slept twelve hours a night solidly for a week, when to the relief of both Hinxman and myself Dr Pennyworth officially discharged me for convalescence at home.

5

My father, Dr Gregory Gordon, MB, BChir, had a general practice in a popular South Coast town, where we had lived as long as I could remember in an over-large Edwardian villa looking across the roofs of innumerable boarding-houses towards the sea. He too was a St Swithin's man, having qualified there about thirty years before I did. Since then he had been occupied in building a prosperous practice, and was now beginning to suffer success. The hourly ringing of doorbell and telephone were as natural a part of my childhood as the chiming of the grandfather clock below the stairs; but in those days my father still had time to read textbooks and occasionally take me to the County ground, while now that his patients included not only the Mayor but most of the Corporation and the Chamber of Commerce as well, he had barely a moment to sit down with the *Lancet* or glance at the cricket scores. Even as I arrived home the next afternoon I met him dashing from the front door with his bag.

'Hello, Richard my boy! Good to see you. Better?'

'Very much better, thanks.'

'What was it you had? Catarrhal jaundice?'

'Yes, except that nowadays they call it infective hepatitis.'

'You're a bit on the thin side. Sorry I couldn't get up with your mother to see you. They looked after you all right in St Swithin's, I hope? Who was your doctor?'

'Old Pennyworth.'

'Good lord, is he still going? I thought he'd be dead long ago. How are you feeling in yourself?'

'A bit tottery still.'

'You'll soon get over it. As a matter of fact, I was rather hoping you could help me out with a few surgeries a little later on. Must rush off now – I've got a perforation miles away on the other side of the housing estate. Ask Miss Jamieson to make you some tea.'

'Isn't mother in?'

'Mother? I can't remember whether it's her afternoon to help with the Young Conservatives or the Old Contemptibles.' As my mother honoured all the obligations of a successful doctor's wife, she rarely seemed to meet my father at all between his being called away from breakfast to see a suspected appendix to his coming in at midnight from seeing a suspected drunk-in-charge. 'By the way, if any phone calls come in be a good lad and see what you can make of the symptoms. Such a help to Miss Jamieson at this time of the year.'

He then jumped into his car and drove off.

I had hoped during my convalescence gracefully to introduce the subject of Sally Nightingale. Although I had seen little more of her before leaving hospital – and I was conscious that she had seen me only lying on my back with my mouth wide open – the prospect of perhaps one day marrying her now lay on my mind much more excitingly than the prospect of perhaps one day passing my FRCS examination. It would be equally stimulating to my self-esteem, just as useful to my career, possibly easier, and much more fun.

With other nurses I had fancied at St Swithin's my plans never went further than our next outing to the cinema, but with Sally Nightingale I already saw myself looking like an advertisement for an insurance company. My knowledge of marriage, like my know-ledge of medicine, was still dangerously theoretical, and I had taken advantage of Tony Benskin's calling to see me in hospital to ask frankly what it was like. His reply had been, 'Magnificent, old man, simply magnificent!', which I felt was as unreliable as the cry of midwinter bathers, 'Come on in, the water's fine!' This was confirmed immediately by his producing two dozen photographs of John Tristram Benskin, all of which looked to me exactly the same, though the father seemed to find subtle differences in each.

I now wanted to discuss the whole problem of matrimony with my parents, but it is as awkward a subject for a sensitive young man to work into the conversation as a plea for more cash. Another difficulty was never finding my parents together, or even one of them alone for more than a couple of minutes on end. The days slipped past with walks on the pier and rounds on the golfcourse, until it was the night before I was to return to St Swithin's. Then at last I managed to catch my father alone in his consulting-room, where he was telling an anxious mother on the telephone that green nappies in the first month were nothing to be alarmed about.

'Father,' I began, as he put the instrument

down, 'I wonder if I could have a word with you?'

My solemnity surprised him. 'Why, of course, Richard. What's the trouble? Do you want to buy another car?'

'No, it isn't that – though of course I'd love one of the new Austin Healeys if you felt you could raise the wind. But as a matter of fact,' I said sheepishly, 'I've recently been thinking rather seriously about marriage.'

'Have you really, now? Good Lord! I never saw this note Miss Jamieson left on my desk – there's a gallstone colic at the Grand Hotel. So you're thinking of getting married, are you, Richard? What's her name?'

'Florence Nightingale.'

'Come, come, Richard, surely you've got beyond childish jokes–'

'That really is her name, Father. Though everyone calls her Sally.'

'Is she nice?'

'Terribly nice! Wonderful, in fact. Of course, I only got to know her in bed.'

'Good gracious! I know you young people go the pace a bit, but I didn't think you'd be as brazen about it as that.'

'I mean while I was having jaundice.'

'Oh, I see. A nurse, eh? Well, you could do far worse than that. Most of my friends

50

married nurses. I didn't. I met your mother when she had a Pott's fracture on my doorstep. However...' He fiddled with the blood-pressure machine on his desk. 'Don't think I'm interfering in your affairs, Richard – damn it all, you're a registered medical practitioner, and therefore one of the few people legally credited with more sense than the average population – but don't you feel you ought to get to know this girl a little better before you decide to spend the next half-century in her company? You mean you've proposed to her?'

'Not properly, Father. Nothing as dramatic as that. I was only thinking of matrimony in a ... well, a general sort of way. I don't think Sally even knows that I really want to marry her yet.'

He raised his eyebrows. 'Well, I can only hope it comes as a nice surprise.'

'But I really think I *will* marry her one day,' I continued earnestly. 'Of course, I've had plenty of girl friends before – we all had at St Swithin's – but never have I met anyone in which so many delightful feminine qualities have been collected together. You see she's so–'

The telephone rang.

'One second, Richard. Yes? Speaking. Yes.

51

Right, I'll be along in five minutes. Fits somewhere behind the station,' he explained. 'It's an old GPI I've been nursing along for years. Delighted to hear your plans, Richard. We must have a long chat about them. What's her name again?'

'Sally.'

'Sally. Look here, we'll split a bottle over it when I get back from this case. Then you can tell me all about her.'

But after the fits behind the station and the gallstones in the Grand there was an acute retention down the road and a Colles' fracture at the bus depot, so that my father didn't arrive home until one-thirty. As the next morning I had to catch an early train, I left home without discussing my theoretical wife with anyone.

The date of my return to work was fixed less by my physical condition than Sally's impending official three nights off duty, two of which she was dutifully spending with her mother at home in Barnet. As soon as I reached St Swithin's I sent her a note suggesting a meeting the following evening. Taking advantage of my involuntary saving through lying in bed, I had picked a fashionable restaurant in Soho in which a pair of Sicilian brothers carried on their family tradition of banditry. It was a small place, with tables, waiters, and diners so crowded together that it was difficult to eat the establishment's famous spaghetti without it becoming entwined with a neighbour's asparagus. But it had an orchestra of Charing Cross Road gypsies with a fiddler who breathed encouragingly down girls' necks, and I thought it an excellent place to pursue my suit.

I was sitting in the laboratory that morning thinking excitedly of the hours slipping past, when I was surprised to see Hinxman appear. He had not only refused to talk to me since my return to the hospital, but had pointedly got up and left rooms as I entered them. Now he seemed desperate to start a conversation. After making some distracted comments about glucose tolerance curves until the other pathologists were out of earshot, he exclaimed 'She's gone.'

'Gone? Who's gone?'

'Sally Nightingale, of course.' I stared at him.

'But gone where?'

'For good.'

'No!'

'She has. She simply packed up this morning and left the hospital. She dropped her

53

resignation in matron's letter-box as she went past.' He sat down heavily on to a laboratory stool. 'I've just this minute heard it from the staff nurse on Honesty.'

My first feeling was of bewilderment. 'But what on earth did she want to do that for? She seemed so terribly keen on nursing.'

He made a despairing gesture over some samples of stomach contents. 'It must have been Godfrey, I suppose.'

'Godfrey? Godfrey who?'

'John Godfrey. That air pilot she specialled when he was in Honesty with virus pneumonia. She's gone off with him – that's obvious. What other reason could there be for a girl to disappear? They're probably halfway to South America by now. It's either him or that fellow from the BBC who had asthma, or the stockbroker chap in Private Block with the ulcer.'

'But I didn't know anything about these men!'

'Huh! You didn't know anything about Sally. Fine monkeys she made of us, I must say.' He rested his elbows wearily among a batch of throat swabs. 'There are far too many girls in this hospital who imagine a nurse's uniform isn't complete without a couple of housemen's scalps dangling from the belt. And to think,' he added painfully, 'that I actually wanted to marry her.'

I said nothing.

Suddenly Hinxman held out his pink hand. 'Richard, we've been complete and utter fools. I want to give you my apologies about everything. Particularly the enema.'

'Roger, I accept them with humility.'

We clasped hands across a pile of agar plates growing streptococci.

'You're a gentleman,' he said. 'It's been a lesson to me, let me tell you. Never again.'

'And I thought she was such a nice girl.'

'The nicer they seem, the deeper they bite.'

But it was only when I left the laboratory after a busy morning's work that the numbness of my psychological wound wore off and I felt how painful it really was. I found a letter in my room from my mother saying how delighted she was, and asking when I was bringing Sally down to see them.

6

'Women,' sighed Grimsdyke reflectively. 'A creature I once saw described in an American gynaecology book as "A constipated biped with pain in the back".'

'Well, there's one thing,' I told him firmly. 'It's going to be many a long day before I get involved with another one.'

'I only wish I could agree with you, old lad. I really do. But unfortunately it's a striking psychological fact that once a man has made a fool of himself over one woman, he can hardly wait to repeat the performance with another.'

The conversation then lapsed. It was our last night at the hospital we had first entered as students over eight years before, and we were sitting together in a corner of the empty bar of the King George, looking dejected. My final weeks in St Swithin's had not been particularly happy ones. Gossip spreads in a hospital like sand at a picnic, and my companions in the residency had enjoyed chaffing me heartily, while all the nurses bit their lips and giggled every time I went past. Our jobs had come to their inevitable end, and now my old friend Grimsdyke and myself were to part and make our separate professional ways.

'Haven't you any idea at all what you want to do next?' I had asked him a few days previously in the surgeons' room, as he took off his sterile gown after the day's operating list.

'Not in the slightest,' he had replied cheerfully. 'I shall again throw myself on the medical labour market. The happiest times in my life have always been when I was out of work.'

I was concerned, because I felt that Grimsdyke's unusual talents needed careful organization. But I had overlooked his most enviable quality, which generally saw him out of his scrapes and difficulties – a knack of meeting chaps in pubs. A few days after our conversation in the surgeons' room he had run into a doctor called Paddy O'Dooley in Mooney's Irish House off Piccadilly Circus, who discovered that Grimsdyke was a graduate of the Society of Apothecaries of Cork and immediately offered him a locum in his practice in County Wexford. This my friend accepted, and he was leaving from Paddington the morning after our farewell drink in the King George. His only worry was discovering the exact whereabouts of his new post, the letter of appointment being scrawled on the back of a packet of Player's cigarettes which his new employer had pressed into his hand before disappearing into the seductive glare of Piccadilly.

'I'm a bit vague about the whole set-up,' Grimsdyke, confessed, ordering another beer and a tonic water. The gloom of our evening was deepened through Dr Pennyworth's forbidding me to taste alcohol for three months. 'I gather it's really Paddy's old man's practice, which is at the moment being run by a Polish chum of doubtful morals and doubtful qualifications. Still, it'll be a change of scenery. There's a lot of money round there, so I hear – estates and so on. *And no NHS.*'

'You're sure you don't want to go on with anaesthetics? You might have a big future there, Grim. You didn't kill anybody and you kept the operating team amused when things were going badly. Those are the only attributes a successful anaesthetist needs.'

'Ah, a professional stuffist! I really wouldn't have minded specializing in it, I must confess. I rather like messing about with the knobs, and it brings out the artist in me. A good anaesthetist's like a French chef, you know – take some pure oxygen, flavour with a touch of ether, add a *soupçon* of pentothal, mix with pethidine, and serve garnished with gas. But you realize the trouble with anaesthesia as a life work?'

'Surgeons?'

He nodded. 'Charming and erudite chaps most of them, but as soon as they get into their operating theatres their characters change. It's just like other people getting into their cars. And their stories! Even such an amiable bird as old Cambridge insists on telling his five funny ones to each new batch of students. When you're one of the permanent fixtures in the theatre, the laughter comes less blithely to the lips after the eighth or ninth repetition. Has he told you the one about him and old Sir Lancelot Spratt chasing a duke in his pyjamas down Devonshire Place?'

I nodded.

'Well, imagine hearing it regularly once a month for the rest of your life. Not that it's much of a tale to start with. No, I'm afraid anaesthesia is going to lose me.'

'But haven't you thought of trying some

other specialty before burying yourself in Ireland? ENT, for instance? Obstetrics? Or psychiatry, now? That ought to be in your line.'

'I've thought of it all right. But contrary to popular belief, psychiatry doesn't consist of listening to beautiful blondes lying on couches telling you all about their sex life. Before you get to that you have to sweat it out for years with ordinary common-or-garden lunatics. I don't think I'd last long working in a mental institution – they say the medical staff soon get dottier than the patients. No, old lad. Not uncle Grimsdyke's cup of tea. In fact, the whole ruddy National Health Service isn't. Some chaps may like being able to look up the book and see exactly how much cash they'll be getting at the age of sixty, but not me. I've got the pioneering spirit. The only trouble is, these days there's nowhere left to pioneer to.'

'Well... County Wexford might be the start of a distinguished and prosperous career, then?' I suggested hopefully.

'As well it might, Richard. I feel I've got sympathetic vibrations with the Irish.'

'Steer clear of the poteen.'

'And you steer clear of the girls.'

The following morning I packed my books and belongings at St Swithin's, and saying good-bye to my friends went into lodgings in that indistinct part of London known as 'South Ken'. I had chosen for economy a seedy Victorian house which seemed to have every Underground train on the Inner Circle passing immediately under its foundations. As each of the rooms had a ring attached to its gas fire they were called 'flatlets', and were occupied by young women who dashed in at six and dashed out again at six-thirty, students from the hotter parts of the Commonwealth, and several fat fair-haired women who puffed up and down stairs with cigarettes between their lips, carrying cats. Like many similar houses I had occupied as a student in London, it was a place where people seemed to arrive from nowhere, talk to no one, and leave suddenly. Rent was always payable in advance, and the green-baize letter-board next to the bamboo hat-stand in the hall was heavy with official-looking envelopes to former tenants who had gone to the happy lands of no address.

Without the distraction of gainful work, I now settled down to study for the next Primary Fellowship Examination. As the National Health Service pays its junior hospital doctors about the same as its junior hospital porters, my savings were so small that I had to live frugally. I fed mostly on fried eggs and kippers, cooked on the gas-ring in defiance of the grease-spattered notice demanding 'No Frying'. I spent my time reading Gray's *Anatomy* and Samson Wright's *Physiology* and staring out of the window at the forbidding outlines of the Natural Science Museum opposite, until after a few days it became clear that either the Museum would have to move or I should. Perhaps I was still looking at the world through jaundiced eyes, but I soon became unable to concentrate, to feel enthusiastic about the exam, or to see any future in the medical profession at all. Even if I passed my Primary I should have to find a house surgeon's job before taking the Fellowship Final, and the only ones advertised in the *British Medical Journal* seemed to be in large industrial towns which, however useful their population for aspiring young surgeons, didn't strike me as places to spend the summer. After a spell as house surgeon I might be promoted to a surgical registrar, but the step between that and full consultant was as uncertain as the naval one between commander and captain.

I remembered so many registrars fretting into middle age looking hopefully for signs of arteriosclerosis in their seniors that I even began to wonder if I should have taken up medicine at all. But it was far too late for such reflections. An unemployed doctor, unlike an unemployed barrister, is fitted for nothing else whatever. I supposed that a knack of analysing confusing noises at a distance in people's chests would make me a reasonable garage mechanic, and an ability to feel hidden lumps coupled with a smattering of practical psychology might be of use in the Customs, but otherwise I was a national economic loss. Then as the Natural Science Museum showed no signs of shifting, I decided to take my books across London each day for a change of scenery by exercising my rights as a member and working in the British Medical Association building.

BMA House in Bloomsbury is a large, red-brick place standing about midway between the Royal Free Hospital and the National Union of Railwaymen, originally designed as a temple for the Theosophists. Its doorway, barely large enough to take a consultant's Rolls, leads into a pleasant courtyard in which the medical intellectuals responsible for the *British Medical Journal* and the medical politicians responsible for keeping up the doctor's pay can be seen conversing thoughtfully in the sunlight. There is a club room as satisfyingly gloomy as any in St James's, which is decorated with animal heads sent by sporting African doctors and provides desks and writing-paper. As it seems to be used only by provincial practitioners waiting for trains at nearby St Pancras, or surgeons sleeping off official luncheons, I found it an excellent spot for concentration.

I was sitting at my writing-desk one morning about a week later trying to master the perplexing arrangement of tendons and nerves round the ankle, when a voice behind me said, 'Timothy doth vex all very nervous housemaids.'

I spun round in my chair.

'Dr Farquarson!'

Dr Farquarson was Grimsdyke's uncle, with whom I had spent the most pleasant, and probably the most instructive, fortnight of my medical life as assistant in his general practice in the country. He was a tall, lean Scot who wore a stiff wing collar which he considered as much a professional mark as a clergyman's, and for London a dark suit replaced the tweed one that he used impartially for shooting and surgeries. On the whole, he resembled one of Low's old caricatures of Ramsay MacDonald.

'A very useful mnemonic I always found that for the ankle,' Dr Farquarson said. He had the knack of starting conversations with acquaintances as though he had left them only a moment before, 'Not so good as the one giving you the advanced signs of Casanova's infection, of course –

There was a young man of Bombay
Who thought lues just went away
Now he's got rabies
And bandy-legged babies
And thinks he's the Queen of the May.

'Did you know it?'

I laughed, and admitted I did.

'And how's that idiotic nephew of mine?'

'Very well, I gather. You know he's gone to Ireland? He sent me a postcard the other day.' This had shown the main street of a village which seemed to consist of alternate public houses and betting shops. On the back Grimsdyke had scribbled, 'Note Irish town planning. Natives friendly, though much addicted to funerals.'

65

'Ireland, eh? It's about time he decided to settle down and place whatever brains he has got at the service of some unfortunate community. And this anatomical effort,' he added, indicating my open books, 'would be in aid of the Primary Fellowship examination, I take it?'

'Yes, I'm afraid so.'

'Of course, since my day they've gone and anglicized the whole anatomical nomenclature,' he went on. 'Which is a pity because it gives the medical profession at least the appearance of being educated like gentlemen if they can mouth a few Latin words occasionally. I remember the time I found myself asked to say grace at some luncheon or other. I bowed my head and intoned:

'*Levator labii superioris alaeque nasi*, Amen.' A small muscle in the front of the face, you will recall. No one was any the wiser.' Producing a large gold watch from his waistcoat he added, 'Talking of lunch, could you tear yourself away from your studies to listen to me rambling over a meal?' Dr Farquarson enjoyed giving the impression of extreme age, though he could not have been much older than my father. 'I might even be able to give you some tips on how to bamboozle the examiners.'

'Why, I'd be delighted. If we go now we'll still find a table in the members' dining-room.'

'Members' dining-room, rubbish! We'll go to a place I know in Holborn. The last thing I want to do is eat looking at a lot of doctors.'

Dr Farquarson led me to a restaurant in a cellar at the end of a dark alley, in which steaks were cooked on an open fire and customers from the City sat in high-backed chairs like choir-stalls with their bowler hats clustered like bunches of huge black grapes above them.

'So you're still going in for surgery?' he asked in the middle of his mutton chops.

I nodded.

'These days it's no good just doing surgery, y'know. The hairs of specialization are split finer than that. In America, so they tell me, they have a man for the right kidney and another man for the left kidney. I always believe a specialist is a fellow who charges more and more for knowing less and less, and if I had my own time over again I'd become an omphologist.'

I looked puzzled.

'From the Greek *omphos*. A specialist in

the umbilicus.' Dr Farquarson rarely smiled, but his sandy eyebrows quivered violently whenever he was struck by something amusing. 'There can't be many people smitten by diseases of that particular organ, but on the other hand there can't be many people who've made it their lifelong study. Folk would flock from all over the world. That fellow James Bridie once wrote something about it.' He took another sip from his tankard, 'Which brings me to my point. Would you consider going into general practice?'

'You mean as a temporary measure?'

'I mean as a permanent measure.' As I said nothing, he went on, 'I've just changed my pitch. I've done a swap with a fellow called McBurney I knew up at the University – he's had bad luck, poor fellow, going down with the tubercule. So I'm in Hampden Cross now.'

'You mean north of London?'

'That's right. Do you know it? It's in the so-called green belt, which consists largely of a forest of traffic-signs and petrol pumps. But there's pleasant enough country nearby, and there's an old Abbey and a cricket ground to satisfy a man's spiritual needs. They're building one of these new town affairs on top of it, so I'll soon be wanting an assistant – with a view, as they say in the advertisements.'

I hesitated.

'I apologize for asking,' he said quickly. 'You'll be through your Primary this shot, and you'll have your Fellowship in your pocket by Christmas. You'll be in Harley Street soon enough. Then you can be sure of getting some cases from an old has-been like me.'

He spent the rest of the meal talking about Test Matches.

I took the Primary Fellowship a fortnight later. In the days before the National Health Service the examination was conducted for a handful of candidates in the quietly academic atmosphere of a dissertation in a mediaeval university. But as young doctors now enter for it in the same spirit as they back horses in the Grand National, the contest has to be run on sharper lines. The written papers had for once left me reasonably hopeful, and a few days later I was back again in that bleak little upstairs room which is decorated with the particular blend of green and yellow paint so heavily favoured in Britain for mental hospitals, station waiting-rooms, and the surroundings of police courts. Waiting for my oral, I suddenly felt sick of all examinations. I calculated that since childhood I must have sat a dozen of them, including my School Certificate and driving test. As a medical student I had taken them in company with my friends, which gave the ordeal something of the sporting air of a chancy rugger fixture; but now I not only had to face the examiners alone, but I was aware that my next year's salary depended on it.

These depressing thoughts seemed to be occurring to the other occupant of the waiting-room, a sad-looking young man with mauve socks who sat staring out of the window in silence until he said suddenly, 'If you get old Professor Surridge, you'll know if you've failed.'

'Will I?' I asked in surprise. 'How?'

'He always asks people he's decided to plough what the dose of morphine is.'

'A tough examiner, is he?'

'On the contrary, he's very jolly. He's too kind-hearted to keep chaps in suspense until the results come out. My registrar got through last time – sixth attempt – and was so amazed to find himself outside without being asked the fatal question he put his head back and said 'It's an eighth to a third of a grain, sir.'

We sat without speaking for a while, pondering what the kindly Professor and his less considerate colleagues were at that moment asking the candidates across the green-baize tables.

'You from Bart's?' asked my companion.

'Swithin's.'

'I'm Guy's. First shot?'

'Second.'

'I had a go at the Membership last time.' He was referring to the corresponding examination for prospective physicians. 'Damn near passed, too. I thought my long case had a collapsed lung, and I even decided to perform the coin test for good measure.'

'The coin test? That's a bit old-fashioned, isn't it?'

'Oh, yes, it went out with leeches and gold-headed canes. But some of the examiners are pretty old-fashioned, too. Anyway, in this case it proved a most valuable investigation. I had just produced two half-crowns from my pocket to bang together on the chest – as directed in the textbooks – when the patient stuck out his hand and pocketed them, whispering, 'Thanks, Guv, it's a gastric ulcer, actual."

I managed to overcome my surroundings

with a laugh. 'Didn't that see you through?'

'No, worse luck. The next case – the short one – was a heart. Damn it, I diagnosed it perfectly! The patient was sitting up in bed, and I had plenty of time to listen all over his chest. "Patent ductus, sir," I told the examiner, "Quite correct," he said. "Anything else?" And I said, "No."'

This seemed unreasonably unfair. 'But why on earth didn't they pass you?'

'I hadn't noticed that some blighter had cut both his bloody legs off as well.' A bell tinkled, and we made for the examination-room door. 'I hear they've got a bottle with an orange-pip impacted in a parotid duct,' he whispered helpfully as we went in.

I was directed to Professor Surridge, who turned out to be a little pink fat bald man, giving the impression of just having been lifted from a pan of boiling water.

'Well, Doctor,' he said genially, passing me a large bottle. 'What's that?'

'It could be an orange-pip impacted in a parotid duct, sir.'

'Indeed it could,' he agreed. 'But it *is* a cherry-stone impacted in an appendix. Both rare conditions, eh?' He handed me an odd-looking syringe. 'What would you use that for?'

'Syringing ears, sir?' I suggested.

'Better than the last candidate, at least, Doctor. He wanted to inject piles with it. Actually, it's from Clover's chloroform apparatus. Historical interest, of course. Now let us discuss the anatomy of the appendix and its various aberrant positions.'

I soon felt I was doing well. I fumbled an answer about the course of the appendicular artery, and I made a slight error over the muscular structure of the intestinal wall, but if my own critical standards equalled those of the Royal College of Surgeons I thought that this time I should be through.

'You are familiar with Poupart's ligament?' asked the Professor, as we got on to hernias.

'Of course, sir.'

'Ah! But where is Poupart's junction?'

For a second I felt panic. This was an anatomical feature I'd never heard of.

'It's the next station to Clapham Junction,' he said with a chuckle. 'Truly, Doctor. Have a look at the signal box the next time you go to Brighton. And which hospital do you come from, Doctor?' He leaned back in his chair, looking at me benignly.

'St Swithin's, sir,' I said, smiling back.

'Of course, you know how to tell the difference between a Guy's man and a St

Swithin's man, don't you, Doctor?'

'No, sir?' I realized with added excitement that the oral period must be almost over; at last I seemed to have got a toe on the surgical ladder.

'They say a Guy's man always examines his patients with a hand in his pocket,' the Professor continued, laughing.

I laughed, too.

'And they say a St Swithin's man always examines his patients with *both* hands in his pockets,' he went on, laughing heartily.

I threw back my head and roared.

A bell tinkled in the distance. 'By the way,' said the Professor. 'What's the dose of morphine?'

7

'It was a pity about your Primary,' said Dr Farquarson.

We were sitting together in his consulting-room, which like those of all best British doctors had the air of a Victorian gentleman's study and exhibited nothing much more clinical than a bust of Edward Jenner. I had just arrived at Hampden Cross, a pleasant place on the edge of London's saucer, which had once flourished as the last stop for stage coaches but had long ago been overtaken by their destination. Away from the new by-pass it had the cheerfully inconvenient air of any other busy little English town, with the pedestrians and the traffic struggling for possession of the High Street. But there was fortunately an area of quiet grass and gardens near the Abbey, where Dr Farquarson's surgery was contained in a narrow Georgian house. I was relieved to find such agreeable surroundings, as I was likely to spend the rest of my life in them.

'All these higher examinations are a bit of a gamble, I'd say, if that's any consolation,' Dr Farquarson went on. 'I remember when I took the Edinburgh Membership the clinical hinged on whether you could just feel the tip of the patient's spleen or not. Even the examiners disagreed over it. One failed all the candidates who said they could, and the other failed all the ones who said they couldn't. I happened to be in the unlucky bunch.' He scraped out his pipe with the old scalpel he kept on his desk for the purpose. 'Still, it's better to have studied and lost than never to have learnt anything at all. There's a lot to be said for the old Indian habit of putting 'FRCS (Failed)' after your name. And now I suppose you're waiting for me to give you weighty advice on the ways and means of general practice?'

I looked at him expectantly. I was now reconciled to making my career as a GP rather than a consultant surgeon, and I was determined to be a good one. The modern doctor unfortunately comes from his medical school with haughty views on general practice. For six years he is taught by specialists, who maintain at hospital lectures and hospital dinners that the GP is the backbone of British medicine, but never hesitate to dissect the backbone whenever given the chance. The residents of both Harley Street and the house surgeons' quarters are understandably tempted to show their superiority over cases sent single-handed into hospital with the wrong diagnosis, and we thus came to look upon our teachers as infallible and general practice, like the Church, as fit only for the fools of the medical family.

'Looking back over my long years of experience,' Dr Farquarson went on, 'I would say... What would I say? That I can't think of anything in the slightest way useful to a young man with reasonably active intelligence. You'll know most of the ropes from your father. Patients are much the same all the world over, whether you see 'em being ill at the Government's expense in hospital or being ill in their bedrooms at their own.'

'I hope you'll be forbearing for my first few weeks,' I said.

'That's when you'll get most of your work, of course. They'll all want to have a look at you. Even now they're gossiping over their teacups wondering what you're like.' He stretched his long thin legs under the desk. 'I'm converting the little room next door as a surgery for you. I'm sorry I can't put you up in the house,' he apologized. 'My flat upstairs is hardly big enough for all the junk I've accumulated over the years. And anyway you wouldn't want to room with such a senile specimen as me, would you? The other flat is of course occupied by our estimable Miss Wildewinde.' This was the receptionist who had admitted me, a middle-aged woman of the type seen so often in England in charge of dogs, horses, or other people's children. 'Miss Wilde-winde is a lady of intimidating efficiency, as you will shortly find out. She also dwells lengthily on McBurney's professional and personal attributes, which occasionally makes life like marriage to an over-fresh widow. Anyway, living away from the shop means you'll escape a lot of night calls. And this Crypt Hotel place will probably look after you all right.'

My illusions about general practice were lost within a week. My first discovery was that diseases affecting the population of Hampden Cross seemed to have no con-nexion with the ones we were taught in St Swithin's. Many of my patients suffered from easily identifiable troubles of those overstrained systems The Tubes, The

78

Nerves and The Wind, but many others seemed only to exemplify mankind's fruitless struggle against Nature. There were old women who complained of being too fat and young women who complained of being too thin, people who found they couldn't sleep and people who found they couldn't stay awake, girls who wanted less hair on their legs and men who wanted more on their heads, couples anxious for children who couldn't have any and couples who had too many and didn't know how to stop. The rest simply wanted a certificate. I signed several dozen every day, entitling the holders to anything from more milk to less work, and from getting the youngest off an afternoon's school to getting the eldest off his National Service.

'The poor doctor's signature,' observed Dr Farquarson when I mentioned this to him, 'is the Open Sesame to the Welfare State. Folk can't exist these days in a civilized community without it. Did you know there's a dozen separate Acts of Parliament that call for it? I've counted 'em myself.'

'Well, I hope I'm not doing down the national Exchequer,' I said anxiously. I knew the penalties for careless certification from a chilly little notice issued by the General

Medical Council. Mistakenly entitling an applicant for a bottle of orange juice to a free pair of surgical boots might land me in the local Assizes. 'I also seem to be prescribing about twice as many bottles of medicine as are therapeutically necessary.'

'Don't worry, lad. A citizen's bodily contentment for half a pint of coloured water is cheap at the price for any Government. Anyway, once the public's got the idea in their heads that something does them good you'll never get it out – whether it's medicine, milk drinks, or meat extracts, which as you know consist of eighty per cent flavouring with no food value whatever and twenty per cent salt to save them from the putrefaction they so richly deserve.'

Dr Farquarson started filling his insanitary-looking pipe.

'The trouble with this generation is that its environment's outstripping its intelligence. Look at the village idiot – a hundred years ago he sat contentedly on his bench outside the village inn. Someone occasionally gave him a little beer, and someone occasionally gave him a little hoeing. He never got in his own way or anyone else's. But what happens today? He's got to cope with pedestrian crossings, income-tax, football pools, national insurance, welfare workers, and God knows what. As he can't, he either plagues his doctor as a neurotic or they put him inside. Another fifty years and anyone without a working knowledge of nuclear physics will be certified as mentally defective. Oh, it'll be a happy day when there's more of us inside than out. But at the moment the job of general practice is separating the idiots from the ill.'

'I hope I've done so today,' I told him, noticing his eyebrows quivering. 'I think I spotted an early tubercule and an early schizophrenia. I packed them off with notes to the appropriate hospitals.'

'You were right, of course. The tuberculous one would sooner or later infect the family, and the mad one would sooner or later smash up the china. Though I try to keep people out of hospitals as long as possible, myself. They're abnormal institutions. It's often better for both sides if patients are nursed by their own relatives. A man ought to be given a chance to be born at home, and he certainly ought to have a chance to die there. The family gathers round, you know, and it's only right he should feel the event is something of an occasion.'

'Sterility...' I murmured.

'Ah, sterility! In the old days there were plenty of prostatic old gentlemen going about with their catheters tucked in their hat-brims. If you're going to be infected, it might as well be your own bugs. In hospital you'll get someone else's, and penicillin-resistant ones they'll be, too. Still, I'm boring you. Remarkable how senility makes a man ramble, isn't it?'

I thought practice with Dr Farquarson looked like being stimulating.

My enthusiasm for my new life was dimmed only by crossing the peeling portals of the Crypt Hotel. The hotel stood on the other side of the Abbey, and was a typical English boarding-house of the type I had slept in so many nights since first becoming a medical student. There were yellowing net curtains sagging across the front windows, an austere card askew in the transom announcing VACANCIES, a hall containing chessboard lino worn red down the middle, and a picture of shaggy cattle standing uncomfortably with their feet in a Highland pool. There were notices desiring punctuality over meals and settling accounts, and a landlady whose manner suggested that she was summing up the chances of your murdering the lot of them in their beds. But the place had seemed clean enough and the customary smell of cooking rising up the staircase smelt savoury, so I had decided to stay.

I had been given a room the shape of a cheese-dish tucked under the roof, which was filled with a polished brass bedstead and was as awkward to undress in as a telephone box. There was a bathroom next door with plumbing apparently designed by Emmett, and a threadbare sitting-room downstairs containing a curly marble fireplace, a set of *The British Campaign in France and Flanders*, and a picture of a fat female albino peeping through a waterfall entitled 'Psyche In Her Bath Glen Gurrick Distilleries Ltd'. This room was filled nightly with the 'commercials', red-faced men in blue suits who I felt were welcome for ensuring both variety of company and maintenance of the catering standards. The hotel's regulars were composed of faded old ladies and retired schoolteachers. Then there was Mr Tuppy.

Mr Tuppy was the hotel's funny man. I first met him at dinner the day of my arrival, when he entered the dining-room with the self-assurance of Danny Kaye taking the stage at the Palladium and demanded in general 'Is there a doctor in the house?' This simple remark sent everyone into roars of laughter. Sitting at the table next to mine, he tucked his napkin under his chin and continued to make funny remarks about doctors while I tried to concentrate solemnly on the *Lancet*. When he shortly struck up a conversation he expressed overwhelming surprise that I happened to be of the medical profession, but by this time I was clearly established as his straight man.

'Knew a feller who went to the doctor's once,' he told everyone over his steak pie. 'Had a throat complaint. Couldn't talk above a whisper. Our professional friend here will know all about it, eh, won't you, Doctor? Anyway, this feller – went to the doctor, see. Door opened by a beautiful blonde – all right, Mrs Knottage, you won't have to leave the room – where was I? Oh, yes. Door opened by smashing blonde. Feller says in a hoarse whisper, "Is the doctor at home?" Blonde whispers back, "No, he isn't – come on in."'

The old ladies roared loud enough to shake the medicine bottles on their tables, while I tried to raise as good-natured a grin as possible.

'Reminds me of another one,' Mr Tuppy

breezed along, helping himself to more potatoes. 'Chap goes to a psychiatrist – our professional friend here knows what a psychiatrist is, eh? Feller who goes to the Windmill and looks at the audience. Well, chap goes to psychiatrist, see. Says, "Nothing's wrong with me, doctor – only these red beetles and blue lizards crawling all over me." "All right," says the psychiatrist. "But don't keep brushing them all over me."'

Collapse of everyone, including Mrs Knottage. I later unwisely tried to combat Mr Tuppy by telling a joke about doctors myself, but no one seemed to think it at all funny. I made an even bigger mistake in offering some mild chaff to Joan, our anaemic waitress. She accepted from Mr Tuppy a run of innuendo which would have had the proprietors of any teashop telephone the police, but to me she said frozenly she was not that sort at all, thank you, which lowered me even further in the estimation of my fellow-guests. Mr Tuppy also had an annoying habit of appearing for breakfast rubbing his hands and declaring 'Hail shining morn, don't say it's kippers again,' and of raising the special glass of brown ale to his lips every lunch and supper with the expression 'Lovely grub – you can feel it doing you good!' I shortly developed the habit of sitting with clenched fists waiting for these remarks, and it became clear that I should suffer permanent psychological damage unless I shortly made a change of accommodation.

8

When I began to look for other lodgings seriously I had been in Hampden Cross almost three months. By then the shadow of the Abbey was falling noticeably earlier across our doorstep, the draughts in the surgery were finding their old corners, the mornings had the evasive chill prodromal of autumn, and the evenings stepped softly up the streets in mist. My resignation to an existence spent handling the small change of medicine had already turned into enthusiasm, and our partnership began to stride along successfully. To the patients, Dr Farquarson was the wise, conservative physician, though possibly rather outdated; I was the young, dashing doctor, though possibly rather dangerous. Life was busy, but it seemed uncomplicated. Until the morning I was called to see Mrs Tadwich.

The address given by Miss Wildewinde turned out to be a flat over a sweetshop near the main street. I now always followed Dr Farquarson's advice of trying to make the diagnosis before ringing the doorbell, and I stood on the mat deciding from the careless hang of the curtains and the grubby air of the paintwork that I was about to be confronted with an ageing widow with progressive myosis and rheumatoid arthritis. I felt an involuntary spasm of pity and prepared to do my best for her. Then the door was opened by a plump blonde in a pink negligeé.

'Er – Mrs Tadwich?'

'That's right.'

'I'm the doctor.'

She gave a bright smile. 'Come on in, do. I wasn't expecting you so early in the morning,' she explained, deftly flicking a pair of drying nylons from a string in the untidy sitting-room.

'I usually see my new patients first.'

I followed her through the door beyond, and found myself in the bedroom.

'Do you live here alone?' I asked.

'Oh, yes. Mr Tadwich left,' she explained amiably. 'There's a divorce pending. Would you like me on the bed?'

I began to feel alarmed. This was a situation never experienced in the ordered routine of hospital. At St Swithin's we were strictly forbidden to examine any female patient lower than the clavicles without a nurse as a bedside chaperone, and I saw my career ending prematurely in the bleak chambers of the General Medical Council in London. But I decided that it would look foolish if I simply grabbed my bag and hurried out. Besides, I was under an equal moral obligation to examine her, and if I didn't I might land just as ignominiously before the local Executive Committee to have my pay stopped like a naughty schoolboy's pocket-money.

'What's the trouble?' I asked, hoping that it was some complaint wholly free of ethical dangers, like sinusitis or nits.

'It's my heart, Doctor.'

My spirits fell lower. But there is fortunately one refuge for the nervous young practitioner – the cold professional manner. This is a psychological defence mechanism, which explains why so many newly qualified men appear brusque and unintelligible to their equally terrified patients. Assuming an air that went out with broughams and Gladstone bags in Harley Street, I gripped my lapels and declared, 'The heart, madam? And what are the symptoms?'

'Oh, no symptoms.' She lay back on the pillow, more at home in the situation than I was. 'Just the palpitations sometimes, you know. I've got a problem heart.'

'Indeed?'

'Leastways, that's what the specialist said. There's a funny quiver you can feel in the middle of my chest, just here.'

'No other manifestations of the condition, I presume?'

'Oh, no. They said in hospital it doesn't mean any harm. Don't you want to examine me?' She slipped off her nightdress down to the waist.

'An idiopathic condition, eh?' I said steadily. 'Umm. Nothing to cause any alarm, then. And now,' I announced with dignity, 'Let me palpate this vibration in the cardiac area.' I laid the flat of my hand sharply between her breasts, as though swatting a mosquito. Sticking strictly to clinical terms, I admitted loftily 'I certainly feel a distinct thrill.'

'Go on with you, Doctor,' she said, giving me a wink and a poke in the ribs. 'We're all human, aren't we? How about coming round one evening for a drink?'

'You'd better treat her here in the surgery in future,' said Dr Farquarson, his eyebrows quivering violently. 'Or else send me along. That would finish her.'

'But the whole thing was all my fault,' I said bitterly, tossing my stethoscope on to the examination couch. 'I should have had more control of the situation.'

'It's an occupational risk we've got to run. A woman gets bored in the afternoons, whether she lives in Canterbury or in Canonbury. And the doctor's the easiest one she can run after.'

'But it might have led to all sorts of complications with the GMC! I didn't realise how I had to watch my step.'

'You know the working rule, of course? "It's all right to make your mistress into one of your patients, but it certainly isn't all right to make your patient into one of your mistresses."' He scratched his cheek with the tip of a pair of forceps. 'If I had my way, that would be engraved in stone over medical school doorways. It's much more useful than "The Art Is long", not to say much less depressing. But speaking as a comfortable widower, Richard my lad, the best deterrent is a wife of your own in the background.'

I considered this. 'But don't you think that marriage isn't to be tackled as an emergency operation?'

'That's true,' Dr Farquarson agreed. 'Take

your time. But not for ever.'

I sat down in the patients' chair. 'Anyway, who could I marry? I don't know any girls.'

'Come, Richard! Even to my old eyes the streets of Hampden Cross seem full of them.'

'But they're all on other men's arms or the backs of other men's motor-bikes. I don't seem to know any girls these days. Besides, how do I know I'd choose the right one?'

'I'd say pick the one with the nicest legs. It's as reasonable a way of choosing a wife as any.'

I persuaded Mrs Tadwich to let me continue her cardiac investigation in the surgery, where she appeared in a tight black dress, three-inch heels, and two-inch nails. Hitching up her skirt, she started every consultation by discussing her absconded husband in tones suggesting that an intimate bond now existed between us.

'We didn't see *that* type of patient in Dr McBurney's day,' declared Miss Wilde-winde, pointedly opening the surgery windows afterwards.

It was only a day or two after meeting Mrs Tadwich that I first made acquaintance with the family at 'Capri'. This was one of the houses known as 'Tudor style semi-det.', for which British builders developed such a distressing addiction between the wars. I had been called to examine a Miss Porson, and as I approached through a garden of crushing neatness I diagnosed either a middle-aged housewife with an obsessional neurosis, or an under-occupied elderly spinster putting on weight through idleness, chocolates, and gin. But the door was opened by a classical gall-bladder case, a fair, fat, fertile female of fifty, who was wearing a tweed skirt and a pink blouse.

'Miss Porson?' I asked, speculating when she last had her attack of gallstone colic.

'Why, you're Dr Gordon!'

'That's right.'

'I'd have known it the moment I set eyes on you.' I looked surprised, and she added, 'You're so like your father. He looked after my little girl when we were down with the Rotarians only this year.'

'Really? That's most interesting.'

'My husband knew your father from the days when he was studying engineering in London, you know. They had lots and lots of mutual friends among the students.' Knowing the company my father had kept at St Swithin's, this didn't seem much of a recommendation. 'It's my little Cynthia you've come to see,' Mrs Porson went on. 'The poor child's so *very* delicate.'

I followed her upstairs anxiously. My family's clinical honour was clearly at stake, and I wasn't at all well up in children's medicine. 'Cynthia's a very highly strung child,' Mrs Porson whispered outside the bedroom door. 'You will make allowances, Dr Gordon, won't you? Here's the doctor, dear,' she announced, entering. 'Let Mummy do your pillows and make you comfy, now.'

Cynthia turned out to be a pale, dark, subdued, but pretty girl, sitting up in bed in a flowered nightie, and aged about twenty.

'Good morning,' I said, trying not to look surprised. 'And what's the trouble?'

'She's got one of her feverish bouts, doctor,' said Mother, behind me. 'I took her temperature this morning and it was ninety-nine point six. So I said "Off to bed you go, my girl, and we'll get the doctor."'

'Quite. Well, Miss Porson, have you any particular symptoms?'

'She had a headache just above her eyes and buzzing in her ears,' said Mother.

'And do you often get such attacks?' I asked the patient.

'Yes, doctor,' replied Mother immediately. 'About every six weeks. She's *very* delicate, aren't you, dear?'

'I'm not,' murmured Cynthia, her lower lip protruding almost imperceptibly.

'Yes you are, dear,' Mother wagged her finger, with fairly playful reproach. 'Mother knows, dear.'

'There's nothing physically wrong with Cynthia,' I said to Mrs Porson, accepting a cup of coffee downstairs afterwards. 'Her temperature's quite normal by my thermometer.'

'But I know how careful one has to be. Cynthia's so delicate, particularly now the nights are turning chilly.'

'Quite. Has she any job?'

'Oh, no, Doctor! She's such a help to me in the house.'

'I see.' The diagnosis was now becoming clear. As Dr Farquarson sometimes put it, it isn't only the obstetricians who have the privilege of cutting the umbilical cord.

'You know, I think you'd find her general health would benefit from some outside interests.'

'But she's such a shy girl, the poor dear.'

'Has she any boy friends?'

Her mother looked surprised. 'Why ... no, Doctor. No, none at all.' She added quickly, 'It's not that she isn't interested in the opposite sex, of course.'

'I wasn't suggesting that for a moment,' I said with a smile. 'I'll come and see her tomorrow, if I may.'

'You really must have supper with us one evening, Dr Gordon,' Mrs Porson invited from the front door. 'How about next week?'

I wasn't anxious to be involved in the private lives of my patients, but I accepted – partly because of the family connexion, and partly because it would be an evening away from the Crypt and Mr Tuppy. I hoped meanwhile that Cynthia would find some presentable youth to take her to the pictures, because girls who have regular dates with young men don't develop regular headaches.

The supper was a dismal meal. Mr Porson, who seemed to be some sort of iron merchant, talked only about business. Mrs Porson talked only about her daughter's health. Cynthia talked about nothing at all.

After the meal I suddenly found myself alone with her in the sitting-room. She seemed a pleasant girl, though she appeared to lack all the things mentioned in the advertisements. She hadn't anything to chat about except her symptoms, until she sighed and said, 'I often wish I could go away. For a long, long sea voyage, for instance. I'm sure it would do me ever so much good.'

'Well – why don't you have a try? You might get a job as a stewardess?'

'I've thought of that. But I couldn't really leave Mummy.'

'Perhaps one day the time will come when you'll have to,' I said, as she looked so miserable. 'You know – starting a home of your own.'

She gave one of her rare smiles and began talking about the garden.

'You've done absolute wonders for Cynthia,' whispered Mrs Porson as I left. 'She's *quite* a different girl since you've taken her in hand.'

'I'll tell my father next time I see him,' I smiled back.

'Oh, Dr Gordon,' she breathed. 'Do you really mean it?' I thought this an odd remark, but returned to the Crypt satisfied with my evening's treatment.

'There's another call for Miss Porson,' said Miss Wildewinde the next day. 'We never had anything like so much trouble from that family when Dr McBurney was here.'

This time Cynthia had vague stomach ache. A couple of days later it was vague headache, and three days after that vague earache. Every time Mother took her temperature, packed her off to bed, and picked up the telephone. My work in the New Town was now increasing daily, the influenza virus was jubilantly starting the open season for human beings, and I decided that I must take a firm line. Besides, far from benefiting from my advice, the poor girl was becoming a flourishing neurotic.

After I had examined Cynthia a few days later for a vague backache, I called Mother into the sitting-room and announced as weightily as possible, 'Mrs Porson – I want to have a serious talk with you.'

'Yes, Doctor?'

'About your daughter.'

'But of course, Doctor.' She gave me a smile.

'Mrs Porson, you may think me perhaps rather young and inexperienced–'

'No, no, not at all!' she interrupted. 'Not a *bit* too young. Why, these days young people make up their minds ever so much earlier, don't they?'

'I mean, you may think me rather young to speak to you like this.'

'Say *exactly* what's on your mind, Doctor. I know *just* how you feel.'

'Thank you. Naturally I wanted to mention

it to you before saying anything to Cynthia herself.'

'But how terribly, terribly sweet of you! And they say the younger generation are so inconsiderate.'

'To be blunt, Cynthia needs marriage.'

She threw her arms round me and burst into tears. 'Oh, Doctor! Now *you* can call me mother, too!'

My departure was a blur of Mrs Porson's face, the chintz curtains in the hall, the gnomes in the garden, the white wicket gate... The rest of my rounds passed in a daze.

'But how can the beastly woman possibly have got hold of the idea that I personally wanted to save her blasted daughter from the psychological scrap-heap?' I complained angrily to Dr Farquarson as soon as I got in.

'A doctor's a bit of a catch for any fond mother,' he said, trying to keep his eyebrows under control. 'Though I must admit it's an awkward situation for a young man.'

'But what on earth can I do? And what a fool I've been! I thought even the Porsons couldn't expect me to swallow the medicine as well as prescribe it.'

Dr Farquarson twisted the bell of his stethoscope thoughtfully. 'I'll take over the

Porson household from now on. Though I'm prepared to wager they'll ask for their cards after a couple of visits.'

But even this relief was denied me. The next night Dr Farquarson himself went sick. For several days he had been complaining of 'the screws in the back', and when I returned a syringe to the surgery after a late call I found him stuck in his chair.

'It's only the lumbago,' he explained, rubbing himself painfully. 'Don't you fash yourself, Richard – I'll be as right as rain in the morning.'

'Oughtn't you to see someone?' I asked anxiously. 'I could call up old Rogers. I saw him go into his surgery as I passed.'

'No, no,' he said, with unusual weariness. 'Don't bother him at this hour. He's as over-worked as we are. Besides, I haven't much faith in the medical profession, anyway.'

'Will you let *me* have a look at you, then?' He hesitated, so I added, 'You know you complain yourself about the pig-headed idiots who only go to the doctor feet first.'

'I'm afraid this looks like a slipped disc to me,' I announced a little later.

He sighed and admitted 'Well, now you've said it, that's what I suspected all along.'

'Don't you think you ought to see a

specialist?' I asked with concern. 'I could get you into the private wing at the local hospital. After all, we send them enough patients.'

'Heaven forbid! That place?'

'Look here,' I decided, seeing that I must be firm. 'I'll lay on a car tomorrow and have you run down to London to see Sir Robert Cufford. He knows more about discs than anyone else in the country. Won't you agree to that? Especially as you knew him as a student.'

'And a bumptious stubborn little blighter he was, too.'

'And that's just the type you want, to make you do as you're told. He'll take you into the Royal Neurological and investigate you. I insist on it. It's doctor's orders.'

'But it's impossible, Richard! Who'll run the practice?'

'I will.'

'With the best will in the world, it's too much for one pair of hands.'

'Then I'll get a locum.'

'You won't at this time of the year.'

'I'll try the newly qualified men at St Swithin's.'

'They'll all have got jobs.'

'I'll write to an agency.'

'You never know who they might send.'

We were still considering this problem when the front doorbell rang.

'Damn it!' I said, tired, irritated, and worried. 'That's bound to be some small child with a note saying please send more cotton-wool and some ear cleaners because father's run out.'

On the mat stood Grimsdyke.

9

'Irish medicine's quite unlike medicine anywhere else,' Grimsdyke reflected. 'The chaps don't actually use leprechaun poultices, but there's a cheerful element of witchcraft about it.'

We were in the saloon bar of the Hat and Feathers behind the Deanery the following evening. I no longer visited public houses myself, because a doctor in general practice spotted refreshing himself with half a pint of mild ale is stamped as an incurable drunkard for life. But Grimsdyke had less inhibitions than me about everything, and insisted that our reunion must be celebrated.

Grimsdyke was now our *locum tenens*. That morning I had seen Dr Farquarson off to the Royal Neurological Hospital in London, where Sir Robert Cufford had arranged to take him into the private wing. He had disappeared protesting that he was really much better and warning me of the dangers of having Grimsdyke anywhere near the practice. But Grimsdyke himself, who suffered the chronic delusion that he was the apple of his uncle's eye, seemed delighted to have arrived at such a critical moment.

'You know,' he said warmly, 'I may be flattering myself, but I think I can contribute a lot to the old uncle's practice. On the business and social side, you know. Uncle's a dear old stick, but terribly old-fashioned in his ways. I expect you've found that out? Anyway, until the old chap recovers his health and strength – which I sincerely hope won't be long – you and I, Richard, are going to form one of the brightest partnerships in medicine since Stokes and Adams.'

'Or Burke and Hare,' I suggested. 'Tell me more about Ireland. How did you find Dublin?'

'Just like Cheltenham, except the pillar boxes are painted green. But full of the most amiable coves drinking whisky and water and talking their heads off about nothing very much and telling you how beastly the British were to their aunt's grandmother.'

'But come, now, Grim! Surely that's a stage Irishman?'

'My dear fellow,' he said authoritatively, '*All* Irishmen are stage Irishmen.'

'But what about Irish doctors? After all,

they're one of the most popular exports, next to racehorses. How did you find your professional colleagues down in the country?'

'Ah, my professional colleagues! Outside Dublin things were a bit quainter. I hired a car and went down to Enniscorthy in County Wexford, and put up at Bennett's Hotel while I searched round for my practice. I finally ran him to earth in a pub in that village on the postcard.'

'Doctor O'Dooley, you mean?'

'No, the practice. There was only one patient. He was an old chum called Major McGuinness, though what the devil he'd ever been a Major in except the Peninsular War, I can't imagine.'

'A bit of a waste of medical manpower, wasn't it?' I asked in surprise. 'What became of O'Dooley's father and that Polish fellow you talked about?'

'One was dead and the other had gone off with the pub's chambermaid and started an ice-cream business in Wicklow. Young Paddy himself draws his cash from a brewery or something, and hadn't been seen for months. The Major was the only patient left. He was as fat as a football, and as he'd been pickling himself in whisky since puberty he had bronchitis, arthritis, prostatic hypertrophy, and I

105

think a touch of the tabes as well. He was pretty pleased to see me.'

'I bet he was.'

'Yes,' said Grimsdyke ruefully. 'He couldn't eat his dinner. He'd got toothache.'

I ordered some more drinks, and Grimsdyke went on. 'My first operation was a resounding success. Under the reassuring influence of Power's Gold Label for both of us, I removed the offending molar. Damn neatly, too, I thought.'

'What with? A corkscrew?'

'No, the whole of Paddy's kit, such as it was, was in the Major's house – a great rambling place, like living in the Albert Hall – where Paddy had been lodging for some years. So I moved in too. It was quite simple. You just found some blankets and cooked your own food if you could collect anything to start a fire, and there you were. There seemed to be about a dozen other people doing the same thing, and very odd characters some of them were, too. You kept running into new ones round corners. They didn't seem to know each other very well, but there was usually some whisky knocking about which made for conviviality. The Major was a genial old soul, although the British had apparently been beastly to his aunt's grandmother, too. I settled down quite comfortably.'

As it seemed unlikely Grimsdyke to refuse a job offering no work and free drinks, I asked why he left.

'The practice died,' he explained simply. 'One night the old boy got more bottled than usual, and passed out under the delusion he was riding in the Grand National and the upstairs bannisters were Becher's Brook. Caused quite a sensation, even in that household. Soon the whole village were in. Then we got down to the serious business of the funeral. You've heard about Irish funerals?'

I nodded.

'There hadn't been so much fun in the place since the night the postmistress went potty and took her clothes off in the High Street. I became a figure of great importance, because the old Major, like a good many people, always worried that he'd be good and cold before he was put in his grave. Thought he might wake up again under six feet of earth. All rather morbid. I had to open veins and things, which worried me a bit, because the last doctor I knew who did the same thing jumped the gun and ten minutes later the blood was running down the stairs. Questions were asked at the inquest.'

He took another drink, ruffled even by the recollection.

'Anyway, the old boy was clearly no longer with us. But he'd also been worried about being eaten by worms and so on, and had asked me to fix up some sort of container that would keep him looking in good shape. Until unearthed by archaeologists, I suppose. Fortunately, the local joiner-cum-undertaker was a jovial bird called Seamus, and although he was out of stock in lead coffins we worked out an ingenious method of wrapping the Major in rolls and rolls of lead sheeting, like you put on the roof. Damned expensive, of course, but the Major was paying. Eventually, we boxed him in, there was a good deal of whisky-drinking, and Seamus went round telling one and all that he was going to screw him down. Tears were shed and speeches were made and at last we were ready to move off for the churchyard.'

'I hope,' I said, 'that after such extensive preparations the ceremony proceeded smoothly?'

'It didn't proceed at all. When the moment finally came to leave, we couldn't get the bloody Major off the floor. Absolutely impossible. We couldn't budge him an inch, all lifting. We had a long discussion about it, and decided the only thing was to send for Jim O'Flynn's breakdown van with the crane on it, or to unwrap him again. The guests became divided on this point, and as you know, when Irishmen are divided they become heated. After a while I gathered what I was thought the cause of the trouble, so I slipped away and gathered my few possessions and caught the afternoon bus. And here I am. There wasn't any more point in staying anyway.'

I laughed. 'I don't believe half of that story.'

'It's true. Even I don't have to exaggerate about Ireland. Still, my emerald phase has now passed, Richard. I am to restart as a respectable English GP. And I might say how delighted I am to find myself in practice with an old chum like you.'

'And so am I, indeed!' I clapped him on the shoulder. 'It was always one of my more sentimental hopes at St Swithin's.'

'I'm mugging up my medicine, too. I opened Conybeare's textbook this afternoon at the section on Diseases of The Alimentary Canal. I started with Oral Sepsis and got as far as Disorders of the Salivary Glands by teatime. I should be down to the caecum and appendix by Saturday.'

Grimsdyke's gay demeanour and gay waistcoats certainly came refreshingly to the practice. His manner was perhaps more suited for the bookies' enclosure than the bedside, but he had the superb gift of being able to draw smiles from anyone between nine and ninety. He was obviously popular with the patients – except the Porsons, where he sportingly went in my stead when Cynthia developed her next vague pains, and was received 'very much like the third-rate understudy appearing at short notice on a Saturday night'. Otherwise, only Miss Wildewinde seemed to take a dislike to my friend.

'A cheeky young man,' she described him to me one morning after he had been with us a week.

'Oh, I don't know, Miss Wildewinde. Dr Grimsdyke has a rather cheerful manner, but he's a serious soul at heart.'

'I'm quite sure that Dr McBurney wouldn't have taken to him for a moment, if I may say so.'

'Come, now,' I said charitably. 'He may attract lots of rich old ladies to us as private patients. Who knows?'

'It seems as if he's started,' she said tartly. 'There's a car outside that doesn't look at all National Health.'

I had just finished my surgery, and opening the front door was surprised to find at the kerb a long, new, black Bentley, with a smart young man with curly hair and a six-inch moustache lightly polishing the windscreen with a Paisley handkerchief.

'Dr Gordon?' he asked, a row of teeth appearing beneath the moustache.

'That's right.'

'How do you do, Doctor?' He shook hands with great affability.

'How do you do?'

'Well,' he continued, a slight pause occurring in the conversation. 'Here's a very great motorcar.'

'Of course,' I agreed. 'There's none better.'

'Not in the whole world. It's got everything, plus.' He gave the bonnet a reverent pat. 'Automatic gearbox, variable suspension, built-in lubrication, sunshine roof, three-tone radio – the lot. A wonderful motorcar. A cigar, Doctor,' he insisted, producing a box of Havanas from the glove locker as I offered my cigarette case. 'Take a few for afterwards.

That's right. A drink, Doctor? The fittings include a cocktail cabinet.'

'I'm afraid I can't touch a drop during the day.'

'I'm Frisby,' he said, producing a card. He was the sort of man you often find yourself next to in saloon bars, drinking light ales and talking about tappets. 'Buckingham Palace Motors, of course.'

I nodded. Car salesmen share with insurance agents and medical equipment manufacturers a quaint belief in the solvency of junior members of the medical profession. I had as much chance of buying the Bentley as the *Queen Mary*, but as I had a few minutes free I agreed when he suggested 'I expect you'd like a spin in the motorcar?'

'That was a delightful experience,' I said gratefully, as we drew up after a run round the Abbey. During this Mr Frisby had pointed out the detailed mechanical advantages of his charge in terms I understood as little as he would have followed an anatomy demonstration.

'Doctor,' he said, 'you're going to be very, very happy indeed with this motorcar.'

'I'm sure I would be,' I agreed. 'Except that I'm afraid there's not the slightest prospect of my being able to buy it.'

He stared at me in amazement.

'It was kind of you to demonstrate it, Mr Frisby,' I said, starting to get out. 'But I don't really want it. Or rather, I can't possibly afford it.'

'But you've bought it!' he exclaimed.

'Bought it?' I began to feel annoyed. 'But how could I? I've never seen the car or you before in my life.'

For a second I thought he was going to take back his cigars.

'Now look here,' he went on, much less affably. 'Is this your signature or isn't it?'

He produced a printed order form from his pocket. It was signed 'G S F Grimsdyke, LSApoth (Cork)'.

'This is nothing whatever to do with me,' I protested. 'I can't imagine how my partner found the money to buy a Bentley, but that's his affair. If you want him, he'll be back in half an hour.'

'Now look here – you're Dr Gordon, aren't you?'

I agreed.

'Well you *have* bought the car. We were instructed to charge it up to your practice.'

'What! But ... but ... damn it! Dr Grimsdyke had no authority whatever–'

'See here, Doctor,' said Mr Frisby, now sounding menacing. 'You can't muck about with Buckingham Palace Motors, you know. I've brought this motorcar all the way from London. I'm a busy man. Not to mention that there's a lot more customers interested–'

'Well, you'll just have to take it back again,' I said sharply. 'There's been a mistake.'

'Mistake, eh? I don't think I like the smell of this, Doctor. You can't pull any wool over the eyes of Buckingham Palace Motors.'

'You can leave the bloody thing here, if you like,' I said. 'But you'll never get paid for it before it qualifies for the Old Crocks' Race.'

By this time our conversation had drawn a small crowd staring through the open windows. I jumped out and ran inside the house. Shortly afterwards I saw Mr Frisby drive his merchandise away, possibly to apply for a writ.

'What the devil's this business about the Bentley?' I demanded, as soon as I saw Grimsdyke.

'Oh, it's come, has it? That's quick service. I only posted the order yesterday.'

'Do you mean you were so insane as actually to try and buy one?'

'Of course, old lad,' he replied calmly. 'Just

what the practice wants. Window-dressing. You know what they say – a successful doctor needs a bald head to give an air of wisdom, a paunch to give an air of prosperity, and piles to give an air of anxiety. A posh car continues the process. Why, that's the only way people judge their doctor. You must have heard dozens of times, 'That feller must be good – he's got a Rolls.' Ever tried to park in Harley Street?'

'But it's ridiculous!' I exploded. 'The thing costs thousands and thousands of pounds.'

'But it's perfectly all right, my dear old lad,' he explained condescendingly. 'We'll get it off the income-tax.'

'Income-tax! Income-tax! Do you know how little we really make in this practice? We couldn't pay for it with our income, income-tax, and post-war credits combined.'

'I must say, you're being a bit of a reactionary,' he said, sounding annoyed as well. 'I think you've been with the old uncle too long already.'

Relations between Grimsdyke and myself remained cool for the rest of the day.

The next morning he unexpectedly wandered into my consulting-room as I was about to start the morning surgery. 'Hello, old lad,' he asked. 'Seen the *Medical Observer* anywhere yet? It's out this morning, isn't it?'

'It usually comes second post,' I explained. I was surprised at this eagerness to get his hands on the weekly medical press.

'Oh, does it? Be a good lad and put it aside for me, will you?'

The *Medical Observer* happened to arrive just as I was starting my rounds. I tore open the wrapper wondering what item was likely to have interested Grimsdyke so keenly. I found it in the correspondence columns.

'To the Editor, Dear Sir,' it said. 'We feel we should bring to your notice our remarkable success treating osteoarthritis with massive weekly injections of Vitamin B. In a series of two thousand cases seen in our practice we have obtained lasting relief with this treatment in no less than ninety-eight per cent of patients. The effectiveness of this therapy in our hands leads us to bring it to the notice of your readers, and we should be interested if others have achieved comparable results. Yours, etc.'

The letter was signed:
'Richard Gordon,
G S F Grimsdyke,
4 Monks Walk,
Hampden Cross, Herts.'

'My dear fellow, don't work up so much steam about it,' Grimsdyke said, when I waved the *Medical Observer* in his face. 'Of course I wrote it.'

'But it's advertising!' I said in horror.

'And damn good advertising, too.'

'But what the hell! It's unethical.'

'Oh, come off it, Richard. Surely you don't believe the old idea that doctors never beat the drum? Why, that's how half Harley Street keeps going. I admit they don't put cards in their windows like the Egyptians saying, 'Dr Bloggings Good For Everything Especially Diarrhoea.' They write to the medical journals pointing out such things in a helpful way. It soon gets to the ears of the general public.' He sat down in the surgery chair and put his feet on the desk. 'Why, the world will be hobbling a path to our door in a week's time. Just think of it! We're made, old man.'

'I'm damn well going to write to the Editor and tell him it's a forgery.'

'Steady on, old lad! No need to get excited.'

'I've never come across such a piece of flagrant dishonesty.'

'Dishonesty? That's not dishonesty, that's

good business.'

'In your mind they seem to be one and the same thing.'

He rose to his feet. 'Are you making reflections on my morals, old man?'

'Yes, I am. You're nothing but a dyed-in-the-wool inconsiderate rogue.'

'Oh, I am, am I? Well you're nothing but a stick-in-the-mud old maid.'

On this note the two doctors separated to attend to their patients.

10

Grimsdyke and I did not speak for some days after that. We communicated only by notes passed between our consulting-rooms by Miss Wildewinde:

'Dr Grimsdyke presents his compliments to Dr Gordon, and will he refresh Dr Grimsdyke's memory as to the dose of *Tinct. Belladonnae?*'

'Dr Gordon presents his compliments to Dr Grimsdyke. It's five to thirty minims, and what have you done with the auroscope?'

'Dr Grimsdyke hasn't got the bloody auroscope.'

'Dr Gordon also wants the multivite tablets back, if you please.'

'Dr Grimsdyke has finished the bottle.'

'My God, what are you treating in there? A horse?' My worries were increased through the commotion of changing digs. It had seemed reasonable for Grimsdyke to move into his uncle's flat, and as two new regulars had arrived at the Crypt and Mr Tuppy had started to tell his stories about doctors all over again I had to go.

Feeling that I could not face another boarding-house, I looked down the Personal column of the local newspaper until I saw an advertisement saying: 'Lady of Refinement shares her lovely home with a few similar as donating guests. Write Miss Ashworth, 'The Lodge', Alderman's Lane.' I decided that 'The Lodge' would at least offer a fresh experience. Although my years at St Swithin's had brought me across all types of landlady from the frankly hypochondriacal to the frankly sexy, medical students don't usually get within sniffing distance of Ladies of Refinement.

'The Lodge' turned out to be a neat villa with a faint air of antiseptic discipline about it, like a military convalescent home. The hall had a polished parquet floor on which a footstep would have stood out as startlingly as Man Friday's, there was a hat-stand starkly bare of hats, a brass gong between a pair of brass bowls, pink-and-green leaded windows, and a fleet of galleons sailing boisterously across the wallpaper. There were also two pokerwork notices saying 'Good Doggies Wipe Their Paws' and 'Who Left The Lights On? Naughty!'

Miss Ashworth turned out to be a small

thin middle-aged woman in glasses, who wore sandals and a dress like those issued to the inmates of mental hospitals.

'You'll be so comfortable here, I'm sure,' she said, fussing me into a small room overlooking the back garden. 'But you *will* be careful of the ornaments, won't you?' She indicated the pieces of glossy china which covered almost every horizontal surface above floor-level. 'They all have such *very* deep sentimental attachments for me.'

I assured her that I would be most careful.

Looking me full in the face she said, 'You remind me so much of a dear, *dear* departed friend. Supper is at six-thirty.' She then softly closed the door and disappeared.

The other refined people turned out to be a disgruntled bank manager called Walters, a thin woman in a sweater who spent all her meals intently reading the *Manchester Guardian*, a serious-looking young man with dirty collars and furunculosis, and more old ladies. We all wished each other good morning or good evening, then sat through our meals in an atmosphere of depressed silence, as though waiting for something nasty to happen.

'Sorry to see you've ended up here,' said Mr Walters morosely when we were left alone after supper, which had consisted of sloppy things in thick china bowls.

'Oh, it doesn't seem too bad,' I said, to cheer myself up. Digs are the curse of higher education. I had been living in one sort or another since I was eighteen, and I was now so sick of other people's houses that even rooms in St James's Palace wouldn't have excited me. 'Been here long?'

'Three years. And I'd move tomorrow if I could raise the energy. Not that there'd be much point. I'm a bachelor, you know, and I've lived in pretty well every lodgings in Hampden Cross by now. I suppose I shall just go on here until I drop dead. Then I'll be able to join one of Miss Ashworth's parties.' I looked puzzled, so he continued. 'Didn't you know that Miss A. communicates with her dead guests nightly? It's sometimes quite difficult in this house to tell who are the living inhabitants and who the defunct ones. No, no, my lad,' he said, shaking his head gloomily. 'You take my advice. Don't unpack.'

It was perhaps these disturbing remarks which led to my absently knocking over a small group of china cats in my bedroom. Hoping that one ornament the less wouldn't be noticed, I carefully collected the fragments and hid them in my suitcase. I was just getting into bed when I carelessly pushed a china seal off the edge of the mantelpiece, and this too I gathered guiltily and hid in my case. Three days later I wondered if my subconscious antagonism to lodgings was being transferred to the ornaments, because I had disposed of a china rooster, a little girl holding out her pinafore, and a dog with big eyes and its lead in its mouth. Miss Ashworth's maid didn't seem to notice, but I was aware that my luggage was steadily being filled with pieces of jagged porcelain.

The hostility between Grimsdyke and myself naturally softened as the days passed. I think that we were both looking for a chance to put out our hands and admit we'd been bloody fools. I had in fact decided to seek him out and suggest we sank our quarrel in a pint of bitter, when I arrived back in the surgery one evening and found our narrow hall filled with steel and red plastic furniture.

'What the devil's all this?' I demanded of the man waiting with the invoice. 'It looks as though we were going to start a cocktail bar.'

'I wouldn't know about that, sir. The other doctor gave instructions to deliver today.'

'Oh, he did, did he? Well, my instructions are to take the lot away again. And what are you doing, may I ask?' I demanded of a solemn-looking man in dungarees screwing something on the broom cupboard door. 'PATHOLOGICAL LABORATORY'? What on earth's the meaning of this?'

Beside him were two other notices, saying ELECTRO-CARDIOGRAPH ROOM and PSYCHOLOGICAL CLINIC. One reading X-RAY DEPARTMENT was already fixed to the door of our downstairs lavatory. 'Take them off immediately,' I ordered.

'Can't do that.'

'Can't? Why not?'

'I've got my orders from the other doctor.'

Before the argument could blossom, we were interrupted by the appearance of Dr Rogers through the open front door. Dr Rogers was a fat man who always seemed to be breathless and perspiring, summer or winter, sitting or running. He was the senior practitioner in Hampden Cross, and though growing into the pomposity almost unavoidable from a lifetime of telling people to eat less and go to bed earlier, he was a friendly professional neighbour. He now seemed in a more heated state than usual.

'Ah, Doctor!' he began, wiping his bald head with his handkerchief. 'Just a word ... if you'll permit ... awkward time, I'm sure.'

'Well I *was* going to take surgery, Dr Rogers.'

'Matter of some importance.'

I showed him into the empty consulting-room and closed the door.

After looking at me with rising embarrassment for some seconds he announced, 'Went to the cinema last night.'

This seemed a thin excuse for interrupting my evening's work, but I said politely, 'A good film I hope?'

'Oh, passable, passable. Can't remember what it was about now. Never can these days. Generally go to sleep. My daughter tells me about them afterwards.'

There was another silence.

'Well, Dr Rogers,' I said. 'I'm certainly glad to hear you had a pleasant evening. Now I'm afraid that I have to get on with the surgery–'

'A medical man's got to be on call,' he announced. 'Any hour of the day or night. It's only right.'

I agreed.

'Wouldn't be doing his duty to his patients otherwise.'

I agreed with this too.

'But ... well... Professional dignity, and so on. Eh? Quite inadvertent really, I'm sure. I'm not saying anything. Very pleased to see you in Hampden Cross. But obviously gossip starts among the others. Advertising, you know. Grave charge.'

'I'm afraid I don't quite follow–'

'Trying to make myself clear. In the pictures. 'Dr Gordon Urgently Wanted' flashed on the screen.'

'What! But that's impossible!'

'Afraid so, Doctor. Right in the middle of the big picture. Ah! Remember now – about an American fellow and another American fellow and some sort of girl.'

'But it must have been a mistake,' I said. 'I wasn't even on duty last night.'

'Mistake, Doctor? Couldn't be. Was on every cinema in the district. Not only that, Doctor, it's been appearing every night of the week. And, so I am to believe, at every separate performance.'

I managed to show him out without seizing a scalpel from the suture tray and searching for Grimsdyke. I ran into Miss Wildewinde coming downstairs, carrying a suitcase.

'Miss Wildewinde! Where are you going?'

'Well may you ask!' she said furiously.

'You don't mean – you're leaving us?'

'That's natural enough, surely? As I have been discharged.'

'But ... but you can't! Miss Wildewinde,

you can't possibly,' I implored, gripping her arm on the doorstep. 'It was Grimsdyke, wasn't it? Yes, of course it was! He's gone mad, Miss Wildewinde. Mad as a hatter. Insane. Certifiable. He's got no right to, whatever–'

'Take your hands off me, Dr Gordon, if you please. I don't know anything about Dr Grimsdyke's mental state. All I know is that he gave me a month's notice this morning. And to think! All the years I'd been here with Dr McBurney.'

'But Miss Wildewinde! I withdraw it, absolutely and immediately–'

'I wouldn't stay in this practice another second!'

'I'll double your salary,' I said desperately.

'I wouldn't even stay in the same district as Dr Grimsdyke, sane or insane, if you paid me a king's ransom. Goodbye, Dr Gordon. A man will be calling for my trunks.'

'Oh, she's gone already, has she?' asked Grimsdyke calmly, as soon as I tackled him. 'All the better.'

'What the devil do you mean by it?' I demanded, banging the consulting-room desk. 'I've never heard of such mean and miserable behaviour.'

He looked offended. 'Don't get so shiny,

old man. It's all for our own good. Why do you think people travel by airlines?'

'I can't see what that's got to do in the slightest—'

'Because all the airline advertisements show a blonde hotsie welcoming them up their gangway. Simple psychology. And that's what we want,' he went on lightly. 'Get a smasher for a receptionist, and trade'll double overnight. As a matter of fact, I was rather looking forward to interviewing a few to-morrow afternoon. And how do you like the new furniture? It's the American idea. In the States a doctor's surgery really looks like one — all white paint and white trousers and you could do a gastrectomy on the floor. Impresses the patients no end. And of course the patients like to think you've got all the latest gadgets. Hence the door labels. Good idea, don't you think? *Excreta tauri cerebrum vincit* — Bull Baffles Brains.'

'If I'd had the slightest idea you'd be behaving in this criminally irresponsible manner—'

'You don't appreciate what I'm doing for you, old lad,' he said in a hurt tone. 'Why, for the last couple of weeks I've had your name on the screen twice nightly in every flick house in town. Not my idea, of course,' he added modestly. 'Remember Ben Allen and Bob Sawyer in *Pickwick?* They did it by being called out of church. I just brought the technique up to date.'

I sat down heavily on the consulting-room desk. There didn't seem to be anything to say to Grimsdyke. I still faintly believed that he had the best intentions; but his ideas on the legal limitations of salesmanship, if applied to merchandise instead of medicine, would long ago have landed him at the Old Bailey.

'Wouldn't you like a holiday?' I suggested quietly.

'That's very decent of you, old lad, but I've only just come. Anyway, uncle will be back as soon as they've whipped his disc out.'

'Couldn't you just clear off. I'd willingly stand your fare back to Ireland.'

'That's hardly the way to talk to a friend, if I may say so, old lad.'

'I was not aware that you were one.'

'Oh, I see. That's your attitude, is it?'

'It certainly is. And all I can say, Grimsdyke, is that the sooner you realise it the better.'

'A fine expression of gratitude!' he said indignantly, 'If you're trying to tell me I'm not wanted–'

'I can assure you that you're not.'

'I shan't bother you with the trouble of my company any longer. I might tell you, Gordon, that my uncle shall hear of this as soon as I get to Town. If you want to ruin his practice, it's not entirely your affair.'

Half an hour later Grimsdyke had followed Miss Wildewinde to London.

He left a difficult life behind him. Apart from repairing his ethical sabotage and soothing down Buckingham Palace Motors and the furniture shop, I had to run the practice single-handed without anyone to sort out the National Health cards, the telephone calls, or the patients from the waiting-room. I also had a disturbing note from my father saying, 'Got an extraordinary letter from a fellow called Bill Porson I've hardly seen for years. Are you going to marry his daughter Cynthia? Is she the same one as last time? Are you behaving like a gentleman?' In 'The Lodge' I started hiding a bottle of gin in my wardrobe, and I broke a china pixie, two shepherdesses, and an idiotic-looking horse. I felt that I was going rapidly downhill, psychologically and professionally.

11

'It is still beyond me to suggest a locum off-hand,' wrote Dr Farquarson from the Royal Neurological. 'But I think you should really try to get an assistant of some sort or another, otherwise you'll be joining me here. I suspect I shall be another couple of months out of things yet. Bobbie Cufford and his retinue seem unaware of any measurement of time more delicate than the calendar. I saw him again this morning – I regret to say that he has developed a most prosperous-looking stomach, and the bedside manner of a dead halibut – and he seems intent on keeping me out of circulation until the time comes for me to retire for good. They still haven't got their diagnosis. Whether Bobbie cuts or not seems to depend on whether my right ankle jerk can raise a flicker. At least with general surgeons you're in, cut, and out before you've time to draw a breath.

'I was visited yesterday by my nephew, who very thoughtfully brought me a bunch of grapes and borrowed ten pounds. I am sorry that you had your differences. After hearing his story I can only express my heartfelt gratitude for your keeping both of us on the *Medical Register* and out of the *London Gazette*. I have long classified my nephew as a high-grade mental-defective, but I am beginning to feel this too generous a diagnosis. He has gone I know not whither.'

Finding a new receptionist was easier than finding a new locum. A couple of days after Grimsdyke's departure, as I struggled to hold two surgeries single-handed and see fair play in the waiting-room at the same time, a small cheerful-looking redhead of about nineteen pushed her way forward explaining that she had a 'special appointment with the doctor'.

'Well, I'm the doctor,' I said, starting to shut the consulting-room door. 'And I'm sorry, but you'll have to wait your turn with everyone else.'

'No, not you. The other doctor. The one with the bow tie.'

'Dr Grimsdyke has been called away on a long case and isn't likely to return,' I explained.

Seeing her face drop in childlike disappointment, I added, 'I'm Dr Gordon. Is there anything I can do for you?'

'Dr Grimsdyke promised he'd make me his receptionist.'

'Did he?' I said, brightening immediately. 'That's different. There's no reason why I shouldn't keep a promise for him, is there?' She gave a glance which I felt compared me unfavourably with my late colleague. 'If you'd like to join the practice, I assure you it's a most interesting job. Plenty of time to yourself, too. Not to mention being part of the great army struggling against the forces of disease, and so on. Have you tried it before?'

'I can type a bit,' she said. 'I was with Jennifer Modes.'

'How about a change? There's nothing like variety.' She hesitated. 'The other doctor told me there was a free flat as well. He said it would be nice for him to have me in easy reach for emergencies.'

I had hoped to move into Miss Wilde-winde's apartment myself, but I was pre-pared to put up with my present lodgings in exchange for the chance of occasionally being able to get back to them before midnight.

'Of course there's a flat.'

'OK. I'll take the job,' she agreed. 'I'm proper sorry the other doctor isn't still here, though.'

I found her one of Miss Wildewinde's overalls and she started on the spot. Her name was Miss Strudwick, and she was as out of place in the surgery as a fan-dancer in church. But she was a willing helper. She had a chronic sinusitus which made her sniff a good deal, and an irritating habit of saying 'Aren't I a silly?' when she'd done something like spilling a carefully-gathered twenty-four-hour specimen over the lino, or sending a patient to a psychiatrist for a post-mortem report and a request to the coroner about the mental condition of his subject. She had no idea of professional sterility or professional secrecy, but she seemed to like the patients and gossiped affably with them all in the waiting-room. After a few days she even began to mellow towards me.

'Mind, all the girls at the Palais thought Dr Grimsdyke was ever so nice,' she confessed one night after surgery, while I was trying to teach her how to sterilize a syringe.

'That's where you met him, was it?' I always wondered how Grimsdyke had spent his evenings in Hampden Cross. 'Now you make sure the sterilizer is on, so, and wait until the water has come to the boil.'

'Oh, yes. There every night he was, almost. He did the mamba something delirious.'

'You first of all dismantle the syringe into its component parts, thus.'

'Mind, he wouldn't let on he was a doctor to begin with,' she said, giving a giggle. 'But of course I ought to have known from the start. He had such lovely soft hands to touch you with.'

'Then you wrap the barrel of the syringe in lint, like this.'

'Don't you ever go to the Palais, Doctor?'

'I'm afraid I never seem to get the time, Miss Strudwick.'

'Go on – don't call me Miss Strudwick.' She came a little nearer round the sterilizer. 'Everyone calls me Kitten.'

'Er – the plunger is always boiled separately to avoid breakage–'

'You're one of the shy sort, aren't you?' She looked up at me. 'You couldn't say that about Dr Grimsdyke, I must say.'

'And the needles of course are sterilized as quickly as possible to avoid blunting–'

'But you've got ever such nice kind eyes.'

'Threading them through a square of lint for convenient recovery–'

'Wouldn't you like to get a bit more

friendly, seeing as Fate has brought us together?'

'Er – Miss Strudwick. The – er – temperature of the sterilizer has to be maintained at one hundred degrees Centigrade for two minutes–'

Our conversation was fortunately broken by the telephone calling me out to a confinement, and when I got back I was relieved to find that Miss Strudwick's emotions had cooled with the sterilizer.

In the next few days it became clear that Grimsdyke must have been a highly popular partner at the local Palais. Girls looking almost the same as Kitten Strudwick appeared hopefully in the waiting-room every morning, and I could have taken my choice of half a dozen receptionists. But finding a locum seemed impossible. I wrote to the Secretary of St Swithin's Medical School and to a medical employment agency in Holborn, as well as drafting a mildly misleading advertisement for the *British Medical Journal.* I interviewed one doctor, but he was so old that he seemed likely only to add to the number of my patients; another, with a red face and tweeds, not only arrived drunk but seemed to find nothing unusual in it. There was one excellent young man from India who politely told me that I was too young to be his professional senior, and another excellent young man from Inverness who politely told me that he suffered from schizophrenia. I seemed to have struck the hard core of medical unemployment. Whenever I had been out of work and wanted a locum's job myself every practice in the country seemed fully manned, but now that I was in the unusual position of employer I couldn't find any takers. I even began to hope that Grimsdyke would appear again at the front door – as indeed he might have done, with no embarrassment whatever – when I had a letter from the City General Hospital, in the East End of London.

'*Dear Dr Gordon*, (it said)
'*I should be glad if you would consider me for the post of your locum tenens, of which I heard today from Messrs. Pilcher and Perritt in Holborn. I am twenty–three years of age and qualified from the City General last December, subsequently holding the appointment of house surgeon to Mr Ernest Duff. I am now anxious to have some experience in general practice before continuing with surgery, in which I intend to*

137

specialize. Perhaps you would kindly let me know your decision as soon as you conveniently can? I would add that I possess a car.
Yours sincerely,
Nicholas Barrington,
BM. BCh (Oxon)'

I don't think I had read a letter more gratefully since I opened the official envelope after my final examinations. The writer seemed sane, and wasn't young enough to be a glorified student nor old enough to be a chronic drunkard. He sounded a little prim and precise, but that was only to be expected of an Oxford man. He had worked under Duff, who was so surgically eminent as to have two operations named after him. And even at St Swithin's we recognized the City General students as a genially beery crowd like ourselves. Apart from this, the poor fellow's following the will-o'-the-wisp of surgical specialization struck sympathy from my bosom: I felt that it would be nice to work with someone else who had probably failed the Primary too. Wasting no time, I took a risk and telegraphed Dr Barrington saying APPOINTED FORTHWITH COME IMMEDIATELY IF POSSIBLE ACCOMMODATION RATHER

SHORT BUT CAN MUCK IN WITH ME
UNTIL SETTLED STOP WORK HARD BUT
FUN HOPE YOU DRINK BEER
  GORDON

To which I had the reply ARRIVING NOON
TOMORROW STOP YES I DRINK BEER
  BARRINGTON

'Our troubles are over,' I told Kitten
Strudwick happily that evening. 'A Dr
Barrington is arriving tomorrow to help us.'

'Oh, really? I wonder what he'll be like?'

'Soft hands and a kind heart like Dr
Grimsdyke, I expect. So put on your best
pair of nylons.'

'Go on with you! I didn't think you
noticed my nylons.'

'Doctors are trained to be observant, Miss
Strudwick.'

'Yes,' I reflected, relaxing in the surgery
chair comfortably for the first time since Dr
Farquarson's departure. 'It's going to be a
bit of fun to have someone three years
junior to me to kick about. I shall be able to
hold my lapels and say 'Come come, my lad
– can't you spot a simple case of cranio-
cleidodysostosis? What on earth did they
teach you at the General?' Oh, yes, I'll make

139

the poor chap work all right.'

'I really don't know, I'm sure,' she confessed. 'You doctors ain't a bit like what I thought you was. Do you want these prong things put back in the hot water?'

I was unable to meet my new colleague on his arrival the next day, as I expected to be out on my morning rounds until well past one o'clock.

'Tell him to stick his car round the back,' I told Miss Strudwick. 'And I'll be home as soon as I can. Make him a cup of tea, if he looks the tea type. Anyway, I'm sure you can entertain him.'

I struck a difficult hour trying to persuade a house physician to take a pneumonia into the local hospital, and it was almost two o'clock when I returned. I was at once both annoyed and worried to find that Barrington hadn't arrived. It suddenly occurred to me that he'd found a better job and let me down, and I should have to start the dreary advertising and interviewing all over again. At that hour of the day the hall and waiting-room were empty, and Miss Strudwick had disappeared for lunch. The only person in sight was another of Grimsdyke's clinical camp followers.

'I'm very sorry,' I said as I came in. 'But you're wasting your time. The job's filled. Good morning.'

She looked disappointed. I felt rather sorry myself, because she was a small pretty blonde in a black suit, who looked much cleaner than Kitten Strudwick.

'Filled?' She frowned slightly.

'I'm afraid this is really not my responsibility at all. I'm Dr Gordon. If you were led to think there was a job here it's my partner's doing, and he's left for good. It's too bad, but I can't do anything about it now. Good day.'

She gave a quick sigh. 'Well, I'll have to go home again, I suppose?'

'Yes, I'm afraid you will.'

'I must say, Dr Gordon, mistake or not, it's been a good deal of inconvenience coming all this way from the middle of London.'

'The middle of London? Good God! is he offering jobs in all the Palais in London now?'

'I don't think I quite understand?'

'Perhaps you didn't meet Dr Grimsdyke in a dance hall?'

'I have been to a dance hall, certainly. I went to one in Tottenham Court Road last

141

year. And, if you are at all interested, I enjoyed myself very much. But I haven't been with or met a Dr Grimsdyke in those or any less interesting surroundings.'

'But then how on earth did you know that...?'

In my days as a student at St Swithin's I had established a modestly flattering reputation among my companions for imitation of members of the hospital staff. I would often entertain the class with these impressions between theatre cases or while waiting for unpunctual physicians to arrive for ward rounds. Although I could mimic most of the mannerisms of many of the consultants, both my audience and myself agreed that my masterpiece was the hospital's senior surgeon, Sir Lancelot Spratt. Using some cotton-wool for his beard, my impression of his lecture on chronic retention in old men brought laughter from even our most earnest students. I never gave this performance so well as the afternoon I delivered it from the lecturer's rostrum itself, ten minutes before Sir Lancelot was due to occupy it. The laughter of my waiting classmates swelled almost to hysteria as I reached his description of the patient's social difficulties on a picnic. It was at that point that I suspected even my own brilliance, and nervously turning round saw Sir Lancelot observing me with folded arms from the lecturer's entrance in the corner. My feelings of that moment were exactly paralleled in Dr Farquarson's surgery.

'You...' I said, staring at her. 'You ... you're here instead of Dr Barrington?'

'I am Dr Barrington.'

'Dr Nicholas Barrington?' I snatched the letter from my desk.

'*Nichola* Barrington. And it would be rather a coincidence if there were two of us applying, wouldn't it?'

'I'm most terribly sorry,' I gasped. 'I thought you were one of my late partner's popsies. I mean, I thought you were someone else. Oh, God!' I collapsed into the chair. 'What a frightful business! Won't you sit down? Will you have a cup of tea? Have you had lunch?'

'I had some at the local hotel, thank you. I thought I'd better install myself there. Though I'm very grateful for your kind offer of accommodation in the telegram.'

I covered my face.

'You must think me an absolute horror,' I said miserably. 'You see, I hadn't the

143

slightest idea you'd be a woman. I know it's ridiculous, but somehow you always think of a doctor as a man – at least, I do. Oh, God! Why can't they have some term like doctortrix, or something? This is quite the worst thing that's happened to me for years.' I groaned. It seemed the climax of all my troubles. 'How can I ask you to forgive me? Or do you want to walk straight out again?'

But Dr Barrington now seemed to find the situation comfortably amusing.

'Don't worry, Dr Gordon. It's a mistake that's always happening. When I first went to the General I was put down for a rugger trial and a Lodge meeting.'

'I shall never really be able to look you in the face again.'

'I hope you will. Otherwise it's going to make the practice rather difficult isn't it? I've never done any GP before, and I'm hoping to learn a lot.'

'I don't know if I can teach you much. Have you failed the Primary yet? Or haven't you taken it?'

'Oh, I got my Primary when I finished my pre-clinical work at Oxford.' This ripped another fragment from my tattered self-esteem.

'When would you like to start work?' I

asked humbly.

'Any time you like.'

'This afternoon? We're rather pressed.'

'Just give me time to change. I only put this on to impress you – thought you might be a rather overwhelming old man.'

'You know,' I said apologetically, 'I shall never forget this meeting until my dying day.'

I was right.

12

Living professionally with a woman is an
unusual relationship. There were women
students, women housemen, and even
women registrars at St Swithin's, but like
most of the big London teaching hospitals it
was a traditionally anti-feminist institution.
It had refused to take females at all until
obliged to by the grant-paying Government
at the onset of the National Health Service,
and the novelty was greeted with gloom
from all sections of the staff. The
consultants objected because they felt it was
another expression of the general degener-
ation of things (particularly when some
well-intentioned official from the Ministry
pointed out that the bulk of the medical
profession is feminine in Soviet Russia). The
medical school objected, because such
frivolous objects as women would be as out
of place in our leathery tobacco-drenched
common room as in the Athenaeum. The
patients objected because they didn't like
the idea of being 'mucked about by young

girls'. The housemen objected because they would have to behave in the Residency. And the nurses objected because their noses would be put out of joint.

Obstacles were strewn thickly in the new students' path. Would they need chaperones to examine patients in the male wards? (No.) Where would they have their lavatories? (In the old fives court.) Could they join the students' clubs? (They soon ran most of them.) Wouldn't they all get married and have babies before they'd finished the course? (They didn't at RADA.) The first batch arrived, without ceremony, at the start of the new session, and were watched with eager indifference by their established classmates. These were divided into the gloomy ones expecting thick tweeds and thick spectacles, and the even more unbalanced hopeful ones looking for a bunch of smashers. In the end the new students turned out like any other collection of middle-class young women, and within a week no one took particular notice of them. Meanwhile, we had at least the compensation of knowing that the School of Medicine for Women in Gray's Inn Road was now obliged to admit men.

When I left St Swithin's for good there

were still occasional arguments whether women make as good doctors as men. There were certainly no doubts about Nichola Barrington, whose usual name appeared to be Nikki. She was academically sound and clinically practical; she had the knack of managing patients old enough to be her grandfather or young enough to be her boy-friend; and she had a flair for sick children, which pleased me particularly because I have long held that this branch of medicine is the equivalent of veterinary science, and could never join in the mother's delight when the little patient tries to eat the doctor's tie and pukes down his shirt front. My paediatric consultations generally ended in struggles and screams, doubtless laying the foundations of several awkward neuroses in later life, and I was delighted to hand all patients arriving in prams over to my new assistant.

'You seem to be making quite a hit in Hampden Cross,' I told Nikki a few days after her arrival. 'Why, twice today I've been met with disappointed looks and a demand to "see the other doctor".'

'It'll wear off,' she said modestly. 'At the moment they just want to see the freak.'

'I'd hardly call you a freak, Nikki. But I

must say I'm delighted you're getting on so well. Some of the patients can be pretty difficult at first, especially in the New Town. They think it's asserting the rights of cititizenship to be rude to the doctor.'

'Well, I might tell you I was as nervous as a kitten when I started.'

'Of the patients?'

'No. Of you.'

'Of me! Whatever for?'

'In my long clinical career – now stretching over the best part of twelve whole months – I've found that whatever they say about it, men really think they're rather superior to women at medicine and driving cars. But you've been absolutely sweet.'

I laughed. 'By the way, talking of driving…' I started playing with a syringe on the surgery desk. 'I wondered if you'd like to run out to the country tonight for a spot of dinner? We could try the Bull – it's the local beauty spot, you know, horse-brasses round the fire, draughts under the doors, and waiters with arthritis. You don't get a bad meal there. We could ask old Rogers to be on for us both.'

She looked doubtful.

'I thought it would give me a chance to put you wise about the practice,' I continued.

'You know, over the relaxed atmosphere of the dinner-table. Difficult to think of everything in the rush-and-tumble of the surgery.'

'All right,' she agreed. 'Though I must say, when I left the General I didn't expect to be out to dinner again for months.'

Under the mellowing influence of the Bull's roast beef and Yorkshire we talked a good deal. Over the soup I had started by describing the local arrangements for disposing of people going mad in the middle of the night, but we soon started chatting generally about hospitals and housemen, students and sisters, patients and parties.

'What's it like being a woman doctor?' I asked, when the old waiter had gone puffing away over the cheese board.

'My heavens! That's a big question.'

'Or is it a question at all? It's just like being any other doctor, I suppose.'

'Well, it leads to complications some-times.'

'Please spare me the memory,' I said, blushing. She laughed. 'I'd quite forgotten about my arrival. But I think everyone usually falls over backwards to be fair to female doctors. Sometimes you find exam-iners who are a bit fierce with you, but that's only because they're so worried they're being prejudiced in the opposite direction. People make life too easy for us, really. Which is gratifying when you consider what our prototypes were like.'

'You mean Sophia Jex-Blake and her friends, who made such nuisances of themselves in Edinburgh?'

'That's right. Isn't it a pity that there's nothing quite so unfeminine as a feminist?'

'I've certainly known a few qualified battle-axes,' I admitted. 'But you don't look the chained-to-the-railings type yourself.'

'Well, I'm going to stand up for women's rights now. I'm paying for half the dinner.'

'What? Nonsense!'

'There you are – wounded masculine pride. Now you can see what we women are up against all the time.'

'It's not masculine pride,' I insisted. 'It's good manners.'

'Which is often an excuse for the same thing. Women doctors enjoy equal pay, so it serves them right to suffer equal expenses. After all, we only had dinner to discuss the practice.'

I admitted this.

'Then there's another thing, Richard – we want to keep our relationship on a strictly professional basis, don't we?'

I admitted this too.

'I mean, it wouldn't do at all if we didn't?'

'No, not for a minute. Bad for the patients and all that.'

'Good,' she said, reaching for her handbag. 'But if you like I'll let you pay for the tip.'

I realized that Nikki was instinctively right in setting an austerely businesslike stamp on our relationship from the start. Anyway, I asked myself the next morning, what right had I to force my company on such a delightful girl just through the accident of her coming to work in the same place? It occurred to me as I started on my rounds that Nikki had been mixing on equal terms with men since she tore up her gym tunics for dusters, and must by now have collected the cream of the country's manhood in her train. I was no more than a passer-by in the road of life, and in future it was only fair to approach her exclusively on clinical matters.

I happened that evening to get a set of electrocardiograms from the hospital that I particularly wanted to interpret. I always had as much difficulty over the squiggles of the P-Q-R-S-T waves set up by the heartbeat as over the evasive shadows on X-rays, and all I could remember about them from my teaching was the old cardiologists' joke about 'Always getting a premature P after T'. I sat puzzling over the spiky lines in the deserted surgery until it occurred to me that Nikki might know more about the subject than I did. It was clearly my duty to the patient to call in a second opinion.

'I do hope I'm not disturbing you,' I said as I rang at the door of Dr Farquarson's flat, where I had insisted she lived.

'Not a bit, Richard. I was only working through some old surgery notes. Do come in.'

I was surprised to see the change. Dr Farquarson's tastes in interior decoration ran largely to framed photographs of his old class groups with stamp-paper over the ones who had died, dingy native carvings picked up in his travels, sets of indestructibly-bound classics, and neat piles of the *BMJ* and the *Lancet*. Nikki had put flowers in his pair of presentation tankards and a couple of bright cushions on the sofa, while Ian Aird's *Companion in Surgical Studies* and Gray's *Anatomy* lay among scattered sheets of lecture notes on a new coloured table-cloth.

'I'm terribly sorry to interrupt your work,' I apologized, 'but I've a set of ECGs I'd very much like your opinion on, Nikki.'

'Of course, Richard. Though I can't think my opinion's any better than yours.'

'I must say,' I added admiringly, 'you've brightened up old Farquy's room somewhat. I always thought before it looked like Sherlock Holmes' study in Baker Street.'

'I haven't really done much,' she said modestly. 'But won't you sit down?'

'Do you mind a pipe?'

'Heavens, no! I've been kippered in tobacco since I first went up to Oxford.'

'I think Farquy's impregnated the place pretty thoroughly already, anyway. He has some horrible black mixture made up specially in Dundee. It would do excellently for fumigating mattresses.'

'I must say I sometimes itch to redecorate the place.' She looked round her temporary home. 'It *could* be absolutely lovely. I'd have all that herbaceous wallpaper off for a start.'

'Yes, and I think that mahogany affair with the mirror in the corner's a bit of a mistake, don't you?'

We talked about redecoration for a while, then about flats in general, and about digs and landladies (which we disliked), and living in London (which we enjoyed), and the Festival Hall and the riverside pubs and the Boat Race and the places you could get a good meal in Soho and Espresso coffee bars and Hyde Park in Springtime. Then I was startled to hear the Abbey clock chime eleven.

'Good Lord!' I said, jumping up. 'I've wasted your whole evening, Nikki.'

'Of course you haven't, Richard. I wasn't really concentrating on surgery. Besides,' she smiled, 'wouldn't it be terrible to start work if you didn't feel there was a sporting chance of being interrupted?'

I agreed warmly with this, but I felt that I ought to wish her good night.

'By the way,' she said, as I opened the door. 'You forgot these.'

'Oh, the electrocardiograms! But how on earth did they slip my memory? I'll look them up in the book tomorrow, anyway. Good night, Nikki.'

The next evening I had a difficult X-ray which I thought she could help me interpret, and the one after there happened to be a worrying case of diabetes I felt I ought to discuss. The following night I had to ask her opinion about a child I'd seen in the afternoon with suspected mumps, and the

155

next I thought she could advise me about a couple of septic fingers I was treating. Nikki always made some coffee and put some records on her gramophone, and on the whole we were pretty cosy.

It was about this time that I became aware of some peculiar symptoms. I didn't feel ill – on the contrary, I was in a state known clinically as 'euphoria', in which the subject goes about in an unshakable condition of hearty benevolence. But I was beginning to suffer from anorexia and insomnia – I couldn't eat or sleep – and I kept finding myself undergoing mild uncinate fits, in which the patient lapses into a brief state of dreaminess instead of attending to the business in front of him. Then there were my bursts of paroxysmal tachycardia. My pulse rate would suddenly shoot up alarmingly, whenever – for instance – I had to find Nikki to discuss some clinical problem. I put this down to nervousness springing from my naturally shy character. But the whole symptom-complex was highly disturbing to a mildly introspective young man.

'You've got it bad,' said Kitten Strudwick one morning, between patients.

'I beg your pardon?' I said in surprise. 'I've

got what bad?'

'Go on with you!' She gave me a playful dig with the percussion hammer 'I thought Dr Grimsdyke was fast enough. But as they always say, it's the quiet ones what a girl has to watch.'

'I'm afraid I haven't the slightest idea what you're talking about, Miss Strudwick.'

'Well, whatever next? I never thought I'd have to tell a doctor all about the birds and the bees. Who do you want in now? The old duck with the arthritis or the Colonel with the hammer-toes?'

13

The next morning I arrived in the surgery to find an alarming letter from Grimsdyke. The envelope was postmarked FOULNESS, but the official-looking writing-paper bore no address.

'*Dear old boy*, (it said)
'*Shame forbids me to tell you where I am. Little did I think, in those happy days at St Swithin's, that the Grimsdykes would he reduced to such shifts. But there are compensations. I always thought "Sweet are the uses of adversity" was a damn silly remark, but anguishing in my present chastening surroundings I have had time to reflect. I made an absolute idiot of myself at Hampden Cross, old lad. You should have kicked me out into the street much sooner than you did. I can only ask you to believe that I was full of good intentions and hope that the friendship of our youth will he preserved. Could you possibly manage to fix me up with twenty-five quid? I shall be released from here at dawn on Saturday, and I could meet you in St Swithin's*

for a beer at lunch. Please bring the cash with you.

  'Yours,
  Grim.'

'Good Lord!' I said to Nikki, handing her the letter. 'The poor fellow's been sent to jail, or something.'

'Foulness?' She picked up the envelope. 'I don't know if there's a prison there or not.'

'It's either that, or he's in some sort of mental institution. Poor old Grim! His career's absolutely up a gum tree now.'

Remorse struck me like the taste of some unpleasant drug. I sat at the consulting-room desk and stared gloomily at the prescription pad.

'Don't worry,' said Nikki kindly. 'It may not be as bad as it looks.'

'With Grimsdyke it generally is,' I said. 'And the whole thing's entirely my fault. He's a wonderful chap really, old Grim. We've known each other since my first day at St Swithin's. I remember it well – he taught me how to slip out of lecture-rooms without being spotted from the front. Why, we shared each other's books and beer for years. And now the unfortunate fellow's in jail because I was a bit hasty with him and

159

kicked him out of the first regular job he ever held.'

'If you hadn't,' said Nikki, 'you'd have been spared the trouble of taking me in.'

'Oh, Lord! Sorry, Nikki. I didn't mean for one moment—'

'I'm sure you didn't.'

'It's just that I can't help feeling sorry for poor Grim. I'll have to go down and see him on Saturday. It's the least I can do. Would you mind staying on duty? And I must pop out to the bank now to collect twenty-five pounds. The chap's probably got nothing between him and starvation except the Prisoners' Aid Society, or whatever it is.'

I drove anxiously into London the next Saturday morning wishing that I had allowed more generously for my friend's enterprising spirit. I was also worrying what to say when I called at the Royal Neurological to see Dr Farquarson, who a few days before had finally fallen under the knife of his old classmate.

An Englishman's hospital is his club, and former graduates of St Swithin's often met in the musty students' common room, with its sofas looking as uncomfortable to sit in as horse-troughs and its caricatures of surgeons who had long ago pursued their patients across the Styx. I was early, and sat alone in the corner with *The Times*, reflecting how young the students were getting these days and wondering what Grimsdyke would look like when he appeared. When he did arrive he seemed in sparkling health and as cheerful as ever.

'I thought you'd been run in,' I said immediately.

'Run in? Good God, old lad! The Grimsdykes may have come close to the wind pretty often, but none of them have suffered the disgrace of ever getting caught. What on earth gave you the idea?'

'Your letter, of course. It sounded as if it had been posted from the condemned cell.'

'Ah, my letter. By the way, are you able to oblige with the small loan? Thanks a lot,' he said, pocketing the notes. 'It'll only be till I've found my feet.'

'Now I've lent you the cash you might at least tell me where you've been,' I insisted.

'In view of your opening remarks, perhaps I'd better. Possibly I overdid the pathos a bit. But my dear chap, the surroundings were really getting me down. I've had a fortnight at the Foulness Hospital.'

'What, as a locum?'

'No, as a resident guinea-pig. It's a research

place – you know, where they make you catch measles to see why.'

'Oh, of course, I've heard of it – the unit that Professor MacRitchie runs?'

'That's it. If you want to find out how well you really feel, just go down there for a bit. They're always screaming for volunteers, so it's just as easy to sign on as letting yourself in for seven years in the Army. And a damned sight more uncomfortable, I should think.'

I was puzzled. 'But why on earth did you want to go there? I didn't know you were all that keen on the progress of medical science.'

'I was reduced to it, old lad. A bit *infra dig*, I thought, a doctor becoming a mere bit of research material, but I had no choice. The exchequer was pretty low when I left Hampden Cross, you know. Also, various coves in London were after my blood – hence the twenty-five quid. And I wanted time to think over a little scheme, of which I'll tell you later. I knew Foulness hospitality ran to free board and lodging and five bob a day for cigarettes, and as you're kept in complete clinical isolation even the bailiffs can't get their hands on you for a fortnight. Above all, of course, no work. You just sit on your fanny and wait to sneeze. It seemed just the job at the time, and I wondered why

162

more people didn't do it.'

'I nearly had a go at the place myself once. Quite a few of the chaps went when we were students.'

'Yes, but wait till you've seen the dump. They used it during the war as a survival school, and they haven't had to alter it much. It looks like a concentration camp up for sale as a going concern. There were about a dozen of us, and we were greeted at the gate by old MacRitchie himself. He's a tall gloomy chap with a long nose and a handshake like a wet sock full of cold porridge. He told us that we had to split into pairs and each pair could take one of the huts. I had the idea of coupling up with a nice little piece of goods from Bedford College for Women, but that apparently wasn't the idea at all. So I decided to chum with the fellow standing next to me, who was a quiet sort called Erskine who said he was a schoolmaster.'

'We got on all right at first. We were put in a sort of packing-case bungalow with all mod. cons. The food and the daily beer issue were left at the doorstep, just like the plague of London, and MacRitchie appeared every morning to drop measles virus down our noses. There were a few books, of course, but these ran largely to the *Stock Exchange Yearbook* and novels about chaps doing other chaps in by various means. There was also a draughts board. I never realized,' Grimsdyke said with sudden heat, 'what a damn silly game draughts was. After the first three days, when I was leading in the series by a hundred and six to a hundred and five, we had an argument. Old Erskine said I'd shifted a draught with the edge of my sleeve. I said I hadn't. The discussion widened. Questions of cheating at draughts, whether chaps are gentlemen or not, and the general state of family morals were brought up. With some force, I might add. We didn't actually come to blows, but we spent the rest of the day staring out of opposite windows.'

'I must say, it seems a silly thing to argue about – a game of draughts.'

'Ah, but you don't understand, Richard. The draught squabble was only a symptom. This fellow Erskine – admirable chap that he was, no doubt, and kind and thoughtful to his little pupils – had the most irritating habit of saying "Doncherknow?" The blasted phrase used to explode in his conversation, like land mines. You wondered when the next one was going off. Damned hard on the nerves, you understand. Also he had the most irritating way of holding his teacup with his fingers right round the bottom. If he'd only *done* it every other time, it would have been all right. It was the inevitability of the thing which got you down. Hence the sober reflections expressed in my letter.'

I sympathized with him, remembering the table habits of Mr Tuppy. 'At least, I'm relieved you suffered nothing worse. And I expect he found just as many objectionable habits in you.'

'Good lord,' said Grimsdyke in surprise. 'That didn't occur to me.'

'But couldn't you have gone out for a walk by yourself. Even in the condemned cell you get regular exercise.'

'Oh, yes, they rather encouraged healthy walks, as long as you steered clear of other people. But the weather, old man! Pouring rain and gales for the whole fortnight. And like a fool I forgot my raincoat. I couldn't possibly have gone out. Why, I might have caught a most fearful infection.'

I laughed, and told him, 'May I say how glad I am that this unfortunate experience has anyway led to the re-establishment of diplomatic relations between us?'

'My dear Richard, and so am I. I behaved like a moron, and I'm sorry.'

'No, no, Grim! I was a bit edgy having the responsibility for Farquy's practice on my plate.'

We shook hands.

'Let us cement our reconciliation in the usual way,' he suggested.

'Capital idea!'

We went across the road to the King George.

After the first pint Grimsdyke remarked, 'You're looking full of beans, Richard. Hard work must agree with you, or something. Have you got anyone else to help you?'

I nodded as I slowly filled my pipe. 'I've got a woman doctor, actually.'

He whistled. 'Good God, old man! How simply ghastly for you. I can just see her now – some frightful piece with legs like a billiard-table, who walks like a hay-cart turning a corner. I suppose she's got spectacles and dandruff and knows everything?'

'As a matter of fact, she isn't at all like that. She's one of the best-looking girls I've come across.'

'Really? Then she's ruddy hopeless as a doctor.'

'On the contrary, she's very good. She gets on well with the patients, works hard, doesn't miss a thing, knows all the latest stuff, manages all the sick kids and midder–'

'Look here, old lad.' Grimsdyke suddenly stared at me narrowly. 'Have you got any social life in common with this – this piece?'

'Well I must admit I've taken her out to dinner.'

'Oh yes? You mean you think she's a case of malnutrition, or are you getting soft on her?'

I suddenly decided that there was no point in self-deception over the diagnosis any longer. I had to talk to someone. I drew a deep breath.

'I'm terribly in love with her,' I said. Grimsdyke spilt his beer. 'Think! Think, old lad!' he implored. 'You can't mean it? You can't! Or can you?'

'But it's wonderful,' I continued, as the idea crept through my consciousness like sunshine on a spring morning. 'Nikki's absolutely a girl in a million.'

'But you can't go about the country falling in love with girls at your age!'

'Why ever not? My endocrine system isn't past it.'

'I mean,' Grimsdyke protested hotly, 'you're not an impoverished medical student any more. She'll expect you to marry her.'

'I only wish she did,' I sighed.

Grimsdyke seemed to find words difficult. 'But think what it *means*, old lad! Staring at her every morning over the top of the *Daily Telegraph* for the rest of your life. Listening to the funny noise she makes when she cleans her teeth. Waking up every night and hearing her snore. There's nothing romantic about marriage. Oh, I know all about it. I've lived with a few hotsies in my time. Once you get the sex stuff worked out of your system it's just like the measles place. Think of it, Richard! She probably says "Doncherknow" and holds her teacup all wrong.'

'Nikki does not say "Doncherknow". She happens to be a remarkably good conversationalist.'

'This is terrible,' Grimsdyke went on, wiping his forehead with his silk handkerchief. 'You don't want to get married, I assure you, old man. Not till you're too old to go out in the evenings, anyway. Think of the fun and games you can have yet. Look here – just to restore you to your senses, let's ring up a couple of nice bits of crumpet and all go out together and have a hell of a good party? I don't even mind going back to Foulness to pay for the treat. It would be a useful social service.'

I shook my head, 'I'm afraid I've got to get back to Hampden Cross. I promised Nikki I'd look in tonight.'

'There you are! You might as well be married already. Just because she lets you get into bed with her—'

'She does *not* let me get into bed with her! I mean, I haven't even tried to find out.'

'Then what the hell's the use of rushing back then?'

It was clear that Grimsdyke had given me up for lost. He shortly had to hurry away, throwing more warnings over his shoulder, to meet a chap in a pub in Fleet Street. I went to visit Dr Farquarson in the Royal Neurological in Bayswater.

It was a wonderful day. It had been one of those rare sunlit autumn mornings when the English countryside looks as if it had been specially designed by Mr Rowland Hilder, and now even Oxford Street seemed as carefree as a fairground as I pulled up benevolently at pedestrian crossings and smiled chivalrously to jostling taxi drivers at traffic lights. I had been in love before – I shivered to remember that a few months ago I was in love with Florence Nightingale – but those were just transient attacks compared with the real, florid, full-blown disease I was now suffering. Why, I asked myself as I light-heartedly weaved my way round Marble Arch, should it be Nikki? Was it simply the accident of work throwing us together? I decided there was clearly more to it than that, or I'd long ago have married one of the pretty handmaidens of medicine at St Swithin's. Perhaps it could all be explained biologically. Something in Nikki's arrangement of hereditary genes appealed to something in the arrangement of my hereditary genes, with the eventual object of producing something else with an arrangement of genes suitable for the continuance of the human race. Meanwhile, all the chemicals with impossible formulae that I had tried to learn in biochemistry were pouring out of my endocrine glands like juice from over-ripe oranges, and giving me this delightful outlook on life. Having confessed my condition to Grimsdyke I wanted to tell everyone in sight, even the policeman holding me up at the bottom of Edgware Road. The only person I felt I should keep in the dark was Dr Farquarson, who might lie in bed developing doubts on the efficient running of his practice.

'Wonderful thing, modern surgery,' Dr Farquarson told me, as I found him sitting up in excellent shape, cleaning his pipe with one of the hospital's throat-swabs. 'When they took my appendix out somewhere in the Highlands they stifled me with chloroform and handed me a bucket automatically when I came round. Here a charming young feller came in and pricked me with a needle, and the next thing I knew I was back in bed asking the lass where my teeth were. Now they say I can think about starting work again in a couple of weeks.'

'A couple of weeks!' I said, aghast.

'Yes, and that's not soon enough for me. They don't take long to get you on your feet after surgery these days. It's all the vogue, I hear, to get the patient to push his own trolley back to the ward.'

'But a fortnight!' I exclaimed. 'That's hardly any time at all. After a serious operation–'

'Oh, in Bobbie Cufford's hands it isn't at all serious.'

'I mean ... well, you never know what complications might ensue – fractured vertebrae, meningitis, all kinds of things. I really think you ought to have a rest, Farquy. How about a long sea voyage in the sunshine?'

I became aware that he, too, was looking at

me strangely.

'Well, we'll see,' he said. 'How's this young lady locum getting on?'

'Oh, her? Very well, I think. I don't see much of her outside surgery hours, of course. She seems very competent.'

'Well, Richard my lad, I'll stay an invalid as long as possible. Though even for you I'm not going to stand more than a couple of weeks with my married sister in Swanage.'

Until then I had somehow overlooked that Dr Farquarson was coming back to the practice at all. Perhaps it was the prospect of his return which made me propose to Nikki that evening. Or perhaps it just happened spontaneously. Few amorous young men sit down and think out a speech and look round for a likely spot to lay their bended knee. Most of them happen to be sitting with a girl in the back of a cinema or the top of a bus, and in a couple of seconds somehow find themselves bound to her for life.

I found Nikki alone in the surgery, repacking our midwifery bag from the sterilizer. She was surprised to see me.

'You *are* back early, Richard. But everything's very quiet. Mrs Horrocks popped at lunchtime, without any trouble. Another

172

boy, but she doesn't seem to mind.'

'Nikki,' I said. 'Nikki, I ... that is, you see, I...'

'Are you all right, Richard?' She suddenly looked concerned. 'You seem rather flushed. Are you sure you haven't got a temperature?'

'I'm in wonderful shape, Nikki. Never felt better in my life. Absolutely terrific form. Nikki, you see, I–'

'Ah, I know.' She smiled. 'I'd forgotten you were meeting your old friend. I should have spotted the symptoms.'

'Honestly, Nikki, I've hardly touched a drop,' I protested. 'I may be drunk, but not with alcohol. You see, Nikki, I really must–'

'Oh, these X-rays arrived from the hospital this morning. They're Mrs Tadwich's oesophagus.'

'Nikki!' I said firmly, grabbing the brown-paper packet.

She looked startled. My nerve failed me.

'Yes, Richard?'

'I love you,' I said, as though mentioning that it was raining outside.

There was a silence. Nikki suddenly looked very solemn. We both dropped our eyes and stared at the floor.

'Do you ... do you mind?' I asked timidly.

173

She shook her head. 'I'm terribly, terribly touched,' she whispered.

'Would you ... would you think of marrying me?' For a few seconds there was another silence, broken only by the sound of the surgery refrigerator going through one of its periodical attacks of ague.

She looked up. 'That's really a very serious question, Richard.'

'I know it's serious, Nikki. Terribly serious. But ... well...'

I began to have the same unpleasant feelings I experienced at the end of my viva in the Primary: things weren't going quite as swimmingly as I expected.

'You see, there's a lot of things,' she went on.

'What sort of things?'

'Well ... there's my Fellowship, for instance.'

'Your Fellowship?'

'You may think me stupid, Richard, or heartless, or both. But I swore I'd never marry ... or even fall in love ... until I'd passed it. I'm a bit obsessional, I suppose. But you know what you hear – women wasting everyone's time, going in for medicine and then going off and getting married. I was determined no one could say that about me. But I'm terribly, terribly fond of you, Richard. Do you think me an ungrateful fool? I expect you do. I suppose I'm just a pig-headed little girl underneath.'

'No, not at all,' I said. There was nothing for it but to be as brave as possible. 'I think you're perfectly right. Absolutely, Nikki. I had exactly the same feelings about the Fellowship myself once. I'm sorry. I shouldn't have had the nerve to raise the subject at all.'

We talked a good deal after that. Then I kissed her good night and drove slowly back to my digs. I played cribbage with Mr Walters till midnight and I knocked over two more china ornaments.

'Had a row?' asked Kitten Strudwick a few days later.

'I beg your pardon?'

'You two. Lovers' tiff, I suppose?'

'Miss Strudwick, I am at a loss to know what you're talking about.'

'Go on with you! Why, the way you've been avoiding each other since Monday anyone would think you was both incubating the measles.'

'My relationship with Dr Barrington, if that is what you're referring to, Miss

Strudwick, is strictly and completely professional. I do wish you wouldn't try and invent romance where it doesn't exist. I'm afraid you've been reading too many of the waiting-room magazines.'

'Don't worry, dearie,' she said cheerfully. 'It'll all come right in the end.'

The week had been a miserable one. I didn't visit Nikki in her flat. I didn't take her out to dinner. I saw her only briefly in the surgery, and I spoke to her only formally about medicine. I was short with Miss Strudwick, morose with the patients, forgetful with myself, and I developed a tendency to stare out of the window for long spells at a time. I suppose failure doesn't cross the mind of a young man starting a proposal any more than it occurs to a young man starting a fight, or he wouldn't embark on either. Now I realized in my periods of painful introspection gazing into the street how absurd it was for such a Caliban as myself to ask Nikki, or even any other girl, to marry him. I was simply the un-marriageable type, condemned to spend the rest of my life in digs, probably playing cribbage with Mr Walters until both of us joined Miss Ashworth's floating band of non-paying guests.

'I dunno,' said Kitten Strudwick, interrupting one of my bouts of window-staring a few days later. 'Why don't you give her a whopping great kiss and be done with it?'

'Miss Strudwick,' I said resignedly. 'I cannot try and hide the situation from you any longer. I appreciate sincerely the kind motives behind your advice, but I have to remind you that we're not all playing in the pictures. In real life that sort of thing isn't done. Besides,' I added, 'it wouldn't work.'

'It would work all right with me, I can tell you.'

'Possibly. But not with ... other people.'

'Oh, don't you be so sure. All girls are the same underneath. Look at all them kings and queens you read about in *Everybody's*.'

'You would spare my feelings, Miss Strudwick, if you began to realize – as I do – that Dr Barrington wishes to have nothing whatever to do with me outside our mutual professional interests.'

'Go on with you! Why the poor girl's eating her heart out. I've just been talking to her.'

'What?' I asked in horror. 'You mean you've actually been discussing me with her?'

''Course I have, dear. In a roundabout

sort-of way, mind you. But a girl's got to get it off her chest to someone, hasn't she? Even if it's only to yours truly.'

'I think perhaps you'd better get the next patient in, Miss Strudwick.'

'Okeydoke. Don't forget what I said, though.'

It happened that evening Nikki and I found ourselves together for the first time in several days, through Miss Strudwick abruptly leaving us alone in the surgery.

'How's the work going?' I asked as breezily as possible.

'Work?' She looked up from an intense search through the filing cabinet.

'For the Fellowship.'

'Oh, quite well. Quite well, thank you.'

'Difficult exam, of course, the Fellowship.'

'Yes, it is. Very.'

'Only ten per cent pass, so they say.'

'So they say.'

I fiddled with an ampoule of penicillin.

'I expect we'll see each other before you go next week,' I said. 'To say good-bye, I mean.'

'Yes. Yes, of course. I expect we will.'

At the door she hesitated. 'Richard—'

'Yes?'

'I – er, talking of the Fellowship, I'm having a bit of trouble trying to learn up my pathology. You used to be a pathologist at St Swithin's, didn't you?'

I nodded.

'Could you possibly spare a moment some time before I go – just to come up and run through some blood slides?'

I felt the least I could do after forcing my attentions on the girl was to teach her a little pathology.

'Of course. I'll do anything to help, Nikki. I'll bring up my microscope tonight.'

There are few situations leading to such intimacy between a man and a woman as sharing the same microscope. You have to sit close together, with your heads touching as you take turns to look down the eyepiece, and your fingers keep getting mixed altering the focusing screw's. It happened as unexpectedly as a sneeze. We were calmly discussing the pathology of pernicious anaemia and I was pointing out the large number of megaloblasts at the other end of the instrument, when I looked up and said, 'Oh, Nikki!' and she said, 'Oh, Richard!' and she was suddenly in my arms and I was kissing her wildly and we were going to be married.

14

Nikki and I, like several million others, decided on a 'quiet' wedding. But there is as little chance of planning a quiet wedding as planning a quiet battle: too many people are involved, all with conflicting interests. To the bride, the event seems mainly an excuse for the uninhibited buying of clothes; to the groom, the most complicated way of starting a holiday yet devised. The bride's friends see it as a social outing with attractive emotional trimmings, and the bridegroom's as the chance of a free booze-up. The relatives are delighted at the opportunity to put on their best hats and see how old all the others are looking, and to the parents it comes as a hurricane in the placid waters of middle-age.

It is a shock to any young man when he realizes that his fiancée has parents. I had always seen Nikki as a single star out-glittering the firmament, and it was strange to think that she belonged to a family like everyone else. But my first duty as a betrothed man was to meet them, and this was arranged for teatime the following Saturday on the polite excuse of my coming to ask her father's permission to propose.

'I'm terribly sorry to shoot off so soon after you're back at work,' I apologized to Dr Farquarson before I left Hampden Cross. He had taken my original breathless news with disappointing calmness. But he was the sort of man who on hearing the Last Trump will only demand who's making that horrible din.

'So you're off to be inspected, then?' He gave a quiver of the eyebrows. 'Well, I can think of pleasanter ways to spend a Saturday afternoon, to be sure. I remember when I first faced the parents of my own poor dear wife. She was the daughter of a Presbyterian minister with views. I'd only one suit at the time and I'd just got in from a midwifery case, so I reeked to high heaven of chloroform. Her father had hardly opened the door before he accused me of being at the bottle. I told him that if a man couldn't distinguish the smell of whisky he wasn't fit to preach to Scots parishioners. After that we got along excellently.'

I laughed. 'I expect I shall drop my tea on the best carpet and trip over the cat and give all the wrong opinions on her father's pet subjects.'

'Och, it'll be no worse than your surgery finals. Don't fash yourself.'

Nikki had now left the practice, and I was meeting her for lunch in the West End before driving out to her parents' home at Richmond. Once I saw her again all thoughts of my coming teatime ordeal flashed away. We drove over Kew Bridge in tremendous spirits, our conversation running largely to 'Is my little bunny-wunny quite comfy-wumfy?' 'Of course your little bunny-wunny's quite comfy-wumfy if my big bunny-wunny is,' which proves that everyone becomes slightly unhinged at such times in their lives.

The Barringtons lived in a pleasant white house by the River, and as I stopped in the short drive the door was flung open by a pink-faced young man of about eighteen with whipcord trousers, a check sports jacket, and a pipe the size of some small wind instrument.

'Richard, this is Robin, my young brother,' Nikki said as we got out of the car.

He gave me the look of deep suspicion reserved by men for chaps likely to go off with their sisters.

'Fancy anyone wanting to marry Nikki.'

'Robin, don't be a beast!'

'I thought you'd marry Bill Wharton.'

'Robin!'

Noticing that I looked surprised, he added 'Oh, Bill Wharton was an old friend of Nikki's. Didn't you know?'

'Robin! Really!'

'Anyway, how do you do,' he said, shaking hands powerfully. 'I say,' he went on, indicating my modest saloon car. 'That isn't this year's model, is it?'

'Yes, it is, as a matter of fact.'

He whistled. 'But didn't you know? On that model the back axle always goes after ten thou. You ought to have got one of last year's.'

'Good Lord, does it?'

'I think we'd better go and face the family,' said Nikki, taking my arm.

Bracing myself, I followed her into the house. The Barrington's sitting-room looked like the third act of a domestic comedy when the curtain had just gone up. To the right, a slim dark woman who might have passed as Nikki's elder sister was sitting behind a tea-tray. Centre, his back to the fireplace and hands deep in his jacket pockets, stood Commander Barrington. He was a tall, grey-haired man in a blue suit, who I gathered from Nikki had now given up sailing ships for insuring them. Symmetrically on the left was an older woman in a yellow dress that seemed to be composed mainly of fringes, whom I took to be Aunt Jane. Aunt Jane, Nikki had explained, lived with them and had a secret of amazing complexity. All three were now looking at me with the strained but polite interest shown by parents when their young children appear during cocktail parties with some strange object found in the garden.

'Mummy, this is Richard.'

'So you're *really* going to marry Nikki!' exclaimed Mrs Barrington at once.

'Shush, shush, Connie!' whispered the Commander loudly. 'We're not supposed to know about it yet.'

'Oh! Of course.'

I was introduced all round. Then there was silence, broken only by Robin blowing loudly through his pipe. But the Commander, clearly the man for any crisis, said heartily, 'How about a spot of tea?'

'Milk or lemon?' said Mrs Barrington with great relief.

The British nation is fortunately at its best when overpowering some awkward social situation, whether caused by mutual embarrassment or water suddenly appearing through the dining-saloon deck. The brilliant national ruse of discussing the weather allowed us all to exchange stereotyped phrases while wondering what the devil to talk about next, then the Commander and I maintained a thoughtful conversation on fishing before realizing that neither knew anything whatever about the subject. Aunt Jane started to say something about her tragic life but was silenced by an abrasive glance from Nikki's mother, and Robin found time to tell me that my particular make of watch and fountain-pen were unfortunately those known to collapse inexplicably during use. I made an unfortunate noise drinking my tea and I dropped a cake plate on the poodle, but the occasion wasn't nearly as bad as I had feared. I felt that the Barringtons were relieved to find that at least I didn't lick the jam spoon or suffer from multiple tics.

'I expect,' said Nikki with a meaning look as the cups were being stacked, 'that you and Daddy want to have a word together?'

'A word?' The Commander sounded as if nothing had been farther from his mind. 'Yes, of course. By all means. Anything you like. Perhaps you'd like to step into my cubby-hole, Richard?'

I followed him to a small room on the other side of the house which was filled with books and decorated with pictures and models of ships. The terrifying moment had come at last. The scene was so familiar from comic drawings that now I didn't know how to perform it. Did I stand to attention and ask for the honour of the hand of his daughter? Or did I just make some sort of joke about adding Nikki to my income-tax? Either approach would not only make me look foolish but – as I hadn't taken the measure of the Commander yet – might land me in the Thames.

I caught his eye. I suddenly realized that he was as nervous as I was.

'How about a gin?' he suggested.

'What a good idea, sir.'

'I was afraid you were a teetotaller.'

'Teetotaller? But what on earth gave you that impression?'

'Nikki said you were sober in your habits.'

'Good Lord! I hope she isn't too blinded by love.'

'Wasn't that meal absolutely ghastly?' he said, taking a bottle and two glasses from a cupboard. 'Talk about torture by teacups.'

I made some polite remark about the nice cakes.

'The trouble is, women will insist on doing things that way. I hate tea usually. Never eat it. I generally have a cup alone in the potting-shed. Water?'

'Thank you.'

'And didn't you think we were about the dreariest family in creation?'

This remark was not what I had expected. 'But I thought that was what you were thinking about me.'

'You! You looked frightfully composed and superior.'

'If I may say so, sir, that's just what struck me about you.'

'Good God! I've been sweating blood at the thought of this afternoon for a week.'

We both laughed.

'Besides which, you blighter,' the Commander continued, handing me my drink, 'you've done me out of a perfectly good afternoon's golf. Do you play?'

'Yes, I do a bit, as it happens.'

We discussed golf for twenty minutes over a couple more gins, then the Commander stood up and said, 'I suppose we'd better go back to the ladies.'

I re-entered the sitting-room feeling much

better than when I had left it.

'Sorry we've been so long, Connie,' Nikki's father said jovially. 'But we seemed to find a lot of things to discuss. Richard here's coming down one Sunday, and Robin and I'll make up a foursome with old Doc Clark. You'll like Clark, Richard – a good scout, though he does putt like a one-armed fiddler. We'll give you a run for your money all right.'

'It's really very kind of you to invite me.'

'Not a bit. Delighted to see you. Can't tell you what a strain it is, playing against the same old crowd week after week. It might do my game a power of good. Couldn't do it much worse, eh, Connie?'

'What did father say?' whispered Nikki, beside me on the sofa.

'Say? What about?'

'About *us*, of course.'

'Good Lord, Nikki! As a matter of fact, I completely forgot to ask him.'

None of the family raised the subject again, and in a few minutes we were all discussing where Nikki and I were going for our honeymoon.

'This is my father,' I said, introducing Nikki.

'My dear Sally! How delighted I am to see you at last.'

'Not Sally, Father. I think you've–'

'But how perfectly stupid of me. How are you, Cynthia?'

'Nikki, Father, Nikki. And here comes my mother. Mother, this is Nikki.'

It was the return fixture the following week. Nikki went through it more comfortably than I did. Within ten minutes she was sitting close to my mother by the fire, cosily discussing the technical details of wedding-dresses.

'But I *must* show you these, Nikki.' My mother suddenly produced a large leather-bound scrap-book from her bureau. I viewed this with intense alarm. I had for years suspected its existence in the house, like some unpleasant family ghost, but I had hoped that it would never be materialized in my presence.

'Not that, Mother!' I cried.

'Why ever not, Richard? Nikki will be terribly interested. The first ones aren't very good,' she explained, opening the pages. 'That was taken when he was three months. Wasn't he sweet, with his little frilly nightie?' Nikki gave a delighted gurgle. 'And this one was when he was two, down on the beach with nothing on at all. And this one–'

'Mother, I'm sure Nikki really isn't at all interested...'

'But I am, Richard, tremendously. And I don't think you've changed a bit. Especially when you've forgotten to get your hair cut.'

'*Didn't* he have lovely curls? Here's the one of him down at Frinton in his little sailor suit...'

I had to sit for twenty minutes while my future wife followed me from infant nudity to my academic gown and rabbit's fur hood, holding my qualifying diploma and sharing a corner of a Greek temple with a palm in a brass pot. I felt this gave her a bitterly unfair advantage in our marriage before it had started.

'If we have any children,' I said, as we started to drive back towards London, 'I'm going to take dozens and dozens of photographs of them and put them in the bank. It's a better way of keeping them in their place than a slipper or a child psychiatrist.'

'But I thought they were lovely, darling. Particularly when you were an oyster in the *Walrus and the Carpenter.*'

I groaned.

'Nikki,' I said. 'If you still want to marry

190

me after that, shall we have the wedding on February the first?'

'In two months' time? But why particularly the first?'

'It'll be a nice easy date for me to remember for anniversaries.'

'Of course, darling.'

'We'll put it in *The Times* on Monday,' I said.

15

'Whom *The Times* hath joined together let no man put asunder,' said Dr Farquarson, as I proudly showed him the page.

'We'd have been top of the column, too,' I said, 'if some blasted Honourable hadn't been allowed to jump the queue as usual. Son of a Socialist peer into the bargain, I shouldn't be surprised.'

'Well, it looks very fine. You know, it's an odd thing, but I hardly glance at the Engagements column myself now. I did when I was a young fellow like you. Then my attention shifted to the Births, and now I suppose I look at the Deaths for my morning's satisfaction. Surprising how you can tell a man's age from the way he opens his newspaper, isn't it? But it'll make your friends sit up over their breakfast all right.'

He had hardly finished speaking when the telephone rang. It was Grimsdyke.

'My dear fellow!' he said in alarm. 'You'll have a hell of a job getting out of it now.'

'But I don't want to get out of it.'

'What? You mean – you actually want to go through with it and marry the girl?'

'Of course I do. I'd do so tomorrow if it was considered decent.'

'But what on earth for?'

'Well, for one thing I'll be able to get out of my digs. Also, I love her.'

'But are you crazy, old lad? You must be! Marriage is a much too serious business to be decided by the emotions. And have you ever actually been to a wedding? Just think of yourself in some beastly reception-rooms off the Brompton Road, with not enough to drink and all the aunts in their best mink tippets and everyone making frightful speeches about going down life's path together and all your troubles being little ones. There'll probably be beastly little boys in pink silk suits, too,' he said with added horror. 'No, no, old lad. Think again. Get a job on a ship and stay out of the country for a couple of years. Remember there's always that useful little escape paragraph underneath saying the fixture will not now take place.'

'I hope the reception won't be too terrible,' I told him. 'Because you're going to have a leading part in it.'

'Me?'

'I want you to be best man, Grim, if you will.'

'My dear chap, I'd lose the ring and get the telegrams all mixed up.'

'Look,' I suggested. 'Nikki's coming out here tonight. If you're free, drive up from Town and we'll all have dinner together.'

After some persuasion he agreed, adding, 'As a matter of fact, old lad, there's a certain little scheme I've started that I'd like to tell you about. I'll come down about seven. It'll be a bit of a treat for uncle. I know the poor old chap's dying to set eyes on me again.'

'My friend Grimsdyke,' I warned Nikki, as the 1930 sports car pulled up noisily outside the surgery, 'is a rather unconventional character. He also has a fertile imagination. I mean, if he should start telling tales of things that used to happen when we were students together, they'll be pure fabrications. A great chap for making up embarrassing stories about people, old Grimsdyke.' I gave a little laugh. 'Not a word of truth in them from beginning to end.'

The doorbell rang loudly.

'Nikki,' I said, 'this is Gaston Grimsdyke, known to one and all as Grim. Grim, this is Nikki.'

I had never seen Grimsdyke put out

194

before. His was such a self-assured character that not even the shock of passing his final examinations had upset him. But Nikki seemed to throw him off his psychological balance. I believe that he really thought I had shackled myself to someone looking like a Russian long-distance runner, and he was flummoxed to find a neat little blonde beside me on the doorstep.

'But, my dear Richard...' he said, rapidly recovering his poise. 'My dear Richard, my heartiest congratulations. Lots of long life and happiness to you both, and so on.' Taking Nikki's hand he bowed low and kissed her knuckles loudly. 'My dear fellow, I *do* congratulate you.'

'Well, Grim,' I said proudly, as nothing flatters a man more than impressing his philandering friends with his fiancée. 'I hope you approve of the bride?'

'Approve? Good heavens, yes, my dear fellow! If I may say so, Nikki, I consider old Richard's taste has improved immeasurably in his old age. When I think of some of those bits you used to go about with at St Swithin's, Richard – I mean, damn it, when I think of ... of...'

'Shall we go straight out to dinner?' suggested Nikki helpfully.

'Delighted.'

Grimsdyke bowed and kissed her hand again.

'If I may use the phrase,' said Grimsdyke, when the three of us were swallowing the Bull's staunchly English coffee, 'you're a very lucky man, Richard.' He reached for Nikki's hand on the tablecloth and patted it in a fatherly manner. 'Nikki, may I say that you are quite the most beautiful and charming girl I've met since I once asked Vivien Leigh for her autograph.'

'Now isn't that sweet of him, Richard?'

'And the thought that old Richard can send you out and make you work as well almost makes me wish I wasn't a confirmed bachelor.'

'I'm really the lucky one,' Nikki told him. 'Don't forget Richard's a confirmed bachelor, too.'

'Ah, yes,' he said, giving her hand another fond pat. 'He won't be able to go round looking at girls' legs anymore.'

'Oh, I don't know,' I interrupted. I felt that Grimsdyke was turning the meal into a *tête-à-tête*. 'He who has plucked the fairest rose in the garden can still admire the stalks of some of the others.'

But Grimsdyke took no notice, and

continued staring into Nikki's eyes. 'I want you always to think of me as an old, old friend of the family,' he said.

'What's this scheme of yours, Grim?' I said forcefully. I was now definitely uneasy. I remembered the time Grimsdyke had neatly charmed away from me a chorus girl from the Windmill, in whom I had already invested most of my quarter's allowance. 'The one you mentioned on the phone.'

'Ah, the scheme, old lad. Yes, of course. I'm a bit of a rolling stone down the avenues of medicine,' he explained to Nikki, still absentmindedly holding her fingers. 'Never will you see Grimsdyke as the dear old GP who's brought half the district into the world and pushed the other half out of it. I'm an individualist, which is a dead loss these days when everyone gets pushed steadily up the NHS ladder, unless you fall off with a coronary on the way. Making a private ladder of your own is somewhat frowned on. Some outside job, like personal physician to an old millionaire with a fondness for travel and no relatives, would suit me down to the ground. Or doctor to some posh hotel – private suite, of course, and use of cellar. But those rackets have been buttoned up long ago. Now at last I've really found something that gives me free-dom of action and limitless opportunity.'

'You're going on an Antarctic expedition?' suggested Nikki.

'Good Lord, nothing *uncomfortable*. Do you remember, Richard, when I was Editor of the *St Swithin's Hospital Gazette?*'

I nodded. This was a slim magazine which appeared in the hospital with the irregularity of fine days in April. The editorial duties were not trying, because its pages contained mostly rugger reports and lectures by the senior staff too dull to be published elsewhere. Grimsdyke took the job not through literary ambition, but because he had heard that the medical publishers trustingly sent a steady supply of free textbooks for review. These Grimsdyke appraised personally, before taking them to the secondhand medical bookseller's round the corner and getting half-price. I remember that I once left my own new copy of Bailey and Love's *Surgery* on the editorial desk while I went to a lecture, and returned to find the book already sold and the review on its way to the printers.

'And a very efficient Editor I was too, if I may say so,' Grimsdyke told Nikki, giving more fatherly pats to her forearm. 'Do you remember my account of old Professor Worthington's funeral, Richard? Real good stuff it was. Bags of dignity. It wasn't my fault the damn fool printer put it under "Sports News". Anyway, on the strength of such experience,' he went on proudly, 'plus a bit of salesmanship, I managed to persuade the cove I met in the Fleet Street pub the other day actually to publish some of my stuff in his paper.'

'What about? If it's racing tips you won't last long.'

'No, no, old lad. I become forthwith "Our Harley Street Specialist", ready to write about anything at the drop of a guinea from scabies to rabies and cardiology to calf's foot jelly.'

'That sounds terribly grand,' said Nikki.

'But aren't you going to find it a bit stiff? Writing like the combined Professors of Medicine, Surgery, and Obstetrics?'

'My dear old lad, don't be silly. Do you suppose those characters in Fleet Street know the slightest thing of what they're writing about? I just go down to the St Swithin's library, take the librarian out for a beer, and curl up with the *British Encyclopædia of Medical Practice.* You pick a nice good morbid subject like hanging or hermaphrodites, and write it out as though you were describing the Cup Final. There you are. The public love it. My first article, as a matter of fact, appears tomorrow morning – a jolly little piece about how to commit suicide, and apparently it's just the sort of stuff they want to buck their readers up over breakfast.' He looked at the clock. 'Good God, I must be going! The paper will be on sale round the Fleet Street coffee-stalls in about an hour's time, and professional that I now am, I'm still bursting to see what it looks like in print.'

'You'll be my best man, then?' I asked, as we stood by our two cars outside the pub.

'My dear old lad, how could I refuse with such a charming girl as Nikki coming to the wedding?' He slipped his arm round her waist and squeezed her tightly. 'Now in view of my official position in the proceedings, may I kiss the bride?' He did so, making quite a noise over it. 'And you *are* charming, Nikki, my dear,' he told her, patting her cheek. 'Much too good for old Richard. As an old friend of the family I shall now also claim the privilege of kissing you good night.'

'Here, steady on!' I said. I now wished that I'd asked Nikki's brother to do the job instead.

Grimsdyke looked round in surprise. 'But it's all right, old man. The best man's allowed to kiss the bride before the wedding.'

'But not too long before. Or too long after,' I added firmly.

We exchanged glances, and for a second we might have had another of our Hampden Cross rows. But Grimsdyke suddenly realized that he was not behaving like a doctor and a gentleman, and Nikki said tactfully, 'Perhaps we'd all better be getting along.'

'Of course.' Grimsdyke put out his hand. 'Sorry, old lad. Understandable enthusiasm. Anyway, Lords Beaverbrook and Rothermere have probably been charging up and down Fleet Street looking for me with chequebooks for the last half-hour. I'll just bid the happy couple good night and push off.'

'Your friend Grimsdyke may be a charming young man,' said Nikki, as we drove away. 'But he's as fresh as a new-laid egg.'

'He had me a bit worried,' I confessed. 'I've seen him in action too many times in the past. He'd just got to the end of his opening manoeuvres.'

'Is that so? Well, I could hardly have slapped his face over the Welsh rarebit. But

I will next time if you like, darling.'

'Oh, don't slap my dear old friend Grimsdyke's face,' I told her. 'Just kick him hard on the kneecap instead.'

'I don't really think he means it,' said Nikki charitably. 'It's just that he looks on life like an excited small boy climbing a big tree.'

'You know, I've often tried to analyse old Grim. And I think you've put your finger exactly on it.'

We drove in silence for a while, agreeably breaking the Highway Code by holding hands on the steering-wheel.

'That's the best man fixed, anyway,' I said. 'We've told the parents, bought the ring, put it in *The Times*, and fixed my holiday for the honeymoon. What else is there to do until they call the banns?'

'To start with,' said Nikki, 'we must really look for somewhere to live.'

16

'I'm not going to *sell* you a house,' said Mr Slivers of Slivers and Sons, estate agents at Hampden Cross. He was a fat, red-faced, tweedy man with the cosy manner of a good GP. 'Oh, no, Doctor. That's not our policy at all. We're going to let you buy one from us. There's no salesmanship about this firm, Doctor. No pressure. We show you the residence and you make up your mind. If you don't like it we won't worry in the least, even though it means showing you every property in Hampden Cross. Cigarette?'

'Thank you.'

'What sort of residence did you have in mind?' he asked.

'A two-roomed flat with central heating,' I said.

'Something detached with at least two bedrooms and a garden for the washing,' said Nikki.

We looked at each other.

'Well now,' said Mr Slivers paternally. 'I'm sure we can find a residence that will satisfy you both. Here are particulars of some most attractive properties, Doctor.' He handed me a sheaf of duplicated sheets. 'Just ask for the keys. Our junior will be pleased to show you round at your convenience.'

There is nothing that brings home to a young man the full seriousness of marriage more than buying a house. I had begun that morning by paying a call on my family's solicitors, Doubleday, Westmoreland, Berridge, and Horsepath in Chancery Lane. These names seemed now to be only window-dressing, the firm being run by a Mr Robbinson, whom I had known since I sat on his knee and listened to his gold watch while he patted me on the head and called me 'the little legatee'. I therefore felt entitled to bounce into his office exclaiming, 'Good morning, Mr Robbinson. I've got magnificent news – I'm going to be married.'

The natural boisterousness of a young man in love was augmented by a crisp January morning and the expectation of meeting Nikki for lunch, and tossing my hat on to a pile of pink-taped papers I continued, 'Absolutely terrific, isn't it? Such a wonderful feeling! The whole of life seems to be going past in Technicolor.'

Mr Robbinson sniffed. The solicitor was a skilled sniffer. When you said anything he doubted, he sniffed with his right nostril; if he disbelieved you, he sniffed with his left; if he thoroughly disapproved as well, he gave you both barrels. He was a tall, thin, white-haired, stooping man with a long nose, who wouldn't have looked out of place standing on one leg in a pond in the zoo. His office, like that of all the best London solicitors, looked like an illustration from *Bleak House*, and he himself sat in a legal mortuary of black tin boxes marked with clients' names and 'Deceased' after them in lighter paint.

'A marriage, eh?' Mr Robbinson always addressed clients in a gloomy undertone directed towards his top waistcoat button.

'That's the idea,' I continued brightly. 'Saturday, February the first, two-thirty at the church. Of course, I've told Nikki – that's my fiancée –all about you, and we'd both be tickled pink if you'd come along. But first of all we're buying a house, and I'd like you to fiddle all the legal stuff for us.'

'You wish me to act for you?' asked Mr Robbinson, sniffing with both nostrils.

A cold draught seemed to rattle the parchment bones of his dead litigation.

'Yes, please,' I said.

Mr Robbinson drew a blank sheet of paper carefully towards him. 'I think you are wise. House purchase has many pitfalls. If the original deeds are not in order you might easily find yourself evicted from the message without compensation.'

'Oh, really?'

'Then there is the inevitable heavy expenditure. You will, I take it, need a mortgage? And I trust you understand that after marriage the income of your wife is added to your own for tax purposes?'

'Yes,' I replied brightly. 'I know that these days the Government are making it so much cheaper for people to live in sin.'

He gave me his three sniffs in succession. 'I will attend to the alteration of your PAYE coding. When did you say was the date of your change in tax status?'

'February the first,' I said, in a subdued voice.

'Have you made a will?' he asked.

'Good Lord! Is it as bad as that? I mean, ought I to?'

'It would be wise. I will draw you a draft will this afternoon. You may have one drawn specifically in anticipation of your marriage, if you wish. Then it can be signed immediately after the ceremony.'

'I think it might be more agreeable all round if I just had an ordinary one to sign here, Mr Robbinson.'

'Very well. It would, of course, be more prudent to make provision in the will for your wife's death as well as your own. Supposing that you were involved in a motor accident on your way back from the church? I will insert a clause stating that she must survive a month longer than you to inherit. Thus we would avoid double estate duty.' Mr Robbinson found little to amuse him in life, but he now gave a laryngitic laugh at the expense of the Inland Revenue. 'Then there is the possibility of issue.'

'Issue? Oh, you mean...'

I saw myself telling Nikki that I was going to pin the nappies on the issue.

'And you will naturally have to make adequate arrangements for the death of the issue, too,' continued Mr Robbinson, warming to his work, 'I would also advise you to take out a life policy for your wife's widowhood. Then there will be the questions of house insurance and sickness benefit. The pitfalls,' he repeated, shaking his head, 'are very, very many. And now as an old friend of the family, may I wish you every happiness?'

'The house agent was better than old Robbinson,' I told Nikki, as we left Mr Slivers' office with the Junior, a lad of sixteen who seemed to have slipped through the fingers of the Lunacy Commissioners. 'This morning I felt like a patient coming in for an operation and being told he'd make a jolly fine post mortem.'

'Poor Richard! You did rather look as though you'd seen your own ghost. I'm sure marriage can't be quite as bad as that.'

'Well, we'll soon find out, won't we? Anyway, we can always cheer ourselves up reading our wills to each other across the fireplace.'

'If we have a fireplace.'

'That's the point. Good lord,' I said, as the Junior stopped outside a large, gloomy, overgrown, mildewy Victorian villa. 'Is this the desirable period residence with many interesting features? It looks more like Borley Rectory in its heyday.'

In the next fortnight we saw a large number of residences, none of which, in disagreement with Mr Slivers, gave us any desire to live in them at all. All we gained was a campaigner's knowledge of house agents' tactics. We soon found that 'A spacious residence' described something big enough to lodge a boarding school, and 'a compact dwelling' meant that the front door opened directly into the parlour. 'An easily run modern apartment' indicated that the owners had left behind their old refrigerator, and 'property capable of improvement' was another way of saying the place was ready for the demolition squad. Anything described as 'suitable for a gentleman' meant that it was criminally expensive, 'very convenient for station' showed that it backed on to the railway lines, and 'an unusual house of character' meant the local eyesore. We began to develop sore feet, frayed tempers, and an envy of the nomadic life.

'If we don't find anything we like this afternoon,' I said, as we rested our tired legs with a pub lunch, 'I'm going to give up the whole idea of a house. We'll try for a furnished flat in some beastly block somewhere in London, and I'll sleep on the surgery couch when I'm on duty.'

Nikki disagreed. 'I want to start with a place of my own. I've lived among other people's furniture far too long as it is.'

I caught her eye. Fortunately, perhaps, I was not so dazzled by love to see that Nikki could sometimes be a highly determined young woman. But knowing my own habits,

I felt that this might not be a bad thing

'All right, darling,' I said. 'We'll carry on the search for Shangri-Là... My metatarsal arches are at your disposal until they collapse.'

'I know exactly what I really want,' Nikki went on. 'A small whitewashed cottage tucked out of sight in a country lane with a garden and a thatched roof and a twisted chimney.'

'And I expect at best we'll end up in a tasteful bijou residence convenient for shops and buses.' I sighed. 'Come along, Nikki. The idiot boy will be waiting.'

The three of us drove in my car between the depressing brick rows on the main road leading away from London. After a mile or so, the Junior stopped staring vacantly through the window and indicated a side turning. Through one of the heartening paradoxes of the English countryside we suddenly found ourselves in a quiet lane winding between tall hedges, looking much the same as when Henry Ford was still playing with his bricks.

'This is it,' said the Junior.

We stopped at a gate in the hedge. Behind the gate was a garden. In the garden was a whitewashed cottage. The roof was tiled, admittedly, but there was a tall twisting chimney.

'I don't *sell* houses,' Mr Slivers repeated, smiling benevolently. 'I only want to help you to buy one.'

'The price *is* rather on the high side–'

He made a sympathetic gesture. 'Alas, Doctor. We have to take our instructions from the vendor.'

'It needs several things doing to it,' said Nikki.

'There is scope for personal touches, certainly,' Mr Slivers agreed.

'Would you mind if we thought it over?' I asked.

'But of course, Doctor. Think it over at your leisure. As long as you like. Never let it be said that we rushed a client into purchasing a property he didn't want.'

There was a knock on the door, and the Junior's head appeared.

'Mr Slivers, the other people wants to know if they can see Floral Cottage at three?'

Nikki and I sat up.

'Other people?'

'Oh, yes,' said Mr Slivers. 'And it's only been on the market since yesterday. Surprising, perhaps, but not with such a desirable

211

rustic retreat. Yes, Herbert, three o'clock will do. Tell them to hurry, because Major Marston will be viewing it at four.'

'Major Marston!' I jumped to my feet. 'You mean that terribly rich chap who owns the brewery?'

'That's quite right, Doctor. I think he is intending to demolish the property and build a large garage. Yes, Herbert, tell the people–'

'One moment!' I felt myself shaking a little. 'Do you think ... is there any possibility ... could you take just a hundred pounds less...?'

'I'm *sure* that can be arranged, Doctor,' said Mr Slivers at once, producing his pen. 'Perhaps you'll let me have a cheque for the deposit? Then you can look upon the property as your own.'

17

Our first reaction to having a home of our own, or at least a ten per cent deposit on it, was to go back and dance in the garden. Then we went through every room, striking matches in the gathering twilight while Nikki delightedly planned the arrangement of our wholly hypothetical furniture. I insisted that I had my old camping kit sent from home and moved in at once, at last saying good-bye to Mr Walters and my digs. Nikki maintained that all men remain as incapable of keeping themselves fed and clean as at six months, but she agreed and later left for London to organize an expedition of her parents.

'Good heavens, you didn't pay all that for *this?*' said her brother Robin, as he smoked his way through our four small rooms next day.

I nodded.

'But didn't you get to know of the Hampden Cross housing estate? The Council are putting one up all the way round here. Heard about it from chap in the City yesterday. Knock the value of the property for six, of course.'

I felt hot and cold sensations travel up and down my spine.

'I hadn't thought of that,' I muttered.

'Then, of course, the value of property's going to drop like a stone next Easter, anyway. All the chaps in the City could tell you that.' He jumped up and down on the bare floorboards. 'I suppose these joists are all right. Did you have the place surveyed?'

'Ought I to have done?'

'Gosh, yes! Why, you don't know what might be the matter underneath.' He gave a deep sniff. 'I shouldn't be at all surprised if that wasn't dry rot.'

It was about this time that I started to sleep badly. My exuberance at joining the landed gentry soon turned into a bleak pessimism that our home was becoming as valueless as an igloo on a hot day. This was particularly serious, because it had now been mortgaged by Mr Robbinson to something called the Spa and Pier Employees' Retirement and Benefit Society. I knew nothing about mortgages except that they were always foreclosed on Christmas Eve in the middle of the third Act, and I had a vision of Nikki and myself barricading the place against hordes of angry pier attendants in peaked caps demanding their money back. Apart from this, the cottage seemed to attract bills as naturally as a herbaceous border attracts bees. I shortly felt that I had staked my savings and my future in something as risky as a string of racehorses, and a little while afterwards I began to wish that I had.

'We'll have to get some builders to do a few things,' said Nikki, as I drove her from the surgery to the cottage a couple of days later. 'Do you happen to know of any?'

I frowned. 'I don't think there's one among the patients, worse luck. It's always a help if you've got some sort of hold on these people.'

'How about those on the corner?'

We stopped the car by a small builders' yard with the notice:

CONTRACTORS
DOGGETT & BUZZARD

'I expect they're as good as any,' I said, as we went inside.

Mr Doggett was a tall, grey, bony man in a

shiny blue suit, behind the lapels of which a pair of serviceable braces peeped coyly. He also seemed to be one of the interesting cases of hat-addiction. Although he removed his bowler in respect for Nikki as we entered, he kept it near him on the desk as we talked and was clearly itching to resume its comforting embrace as soon as we shut the door.

'You leave it all to me,' he said.

'There isn't really much that needs doing,' said Nikki. 'It's mainly a matter of stopping the water coming through the sitting-room ceiling and starting it coming out of the bathroom taps.'

I remembered the magic word. 'Can we have an estimate?' I asked.

'Estimate? By all means, Doctor. Just as soon as you like. I'll bring it round tomorrow afternoon.'

'This estimate thing doesn't look too bad,' I told Nikki over the telephone the following evening.

'What do they want to do to the place, darling?'

'Well, the estimate says 'To well cut out and make good all cracks to ceiling properly prepare line and distemper same bring forward all woodwork the sum of twenty-five pounds'. There's also another ten quid for something I can't understand that has to be done to the cistern. But I don't think it's going to break us.'

'That's wonderful, dearest! When are they going to start?'

'Tomorrow, if we like. Old Doggett says he's putting his three best men on the job. It's a great advantage, this estimate system, isn't it? It lets you know exactly where you are. It's a wonder surgeons don't do it. You know – 'To making six-inch abdominal incision, properly securing haemostasis, clamping, dividing, and ligaturing gastric arteries, removing stomach, fully washing down, making good and suturing firmly with best-quality absorbable catgut, the sum of one hundred guineas.'

Nikki laughed on the other end of the line. 'They'd have to put "Errors and Omissions Excepted", of course. There go the pips again. Ring me tomorrow, darling one.'

Mr Doggett's three best men arrived at the cottage the morning after I had gone into residence myself with a camp bed, a primus, and the surgery oil stove, after burying several pounds' worth of broken chinaware in the garden. There was a tall thin man with a sharp bald head, a long pale face, and the expression of painful despair with mankind seen in paintings of martyred saints; there was a fat jolly man in a striped sweater and an American baseball cap; and there was an old, bent man with long moustaches and bloodhound's eyes, who shuffled slowly about the rooms and was clearly recognized by his companions as being far too senile for work of any sort.

The men greeted me kindly, putting me at ease, then started their day's work. With a private supply of sticks and coal they lit a fire in the bare sitting-room grate, put on a kettle, and settled round reading bits of the *Daily Mirror*.

'Like a cup, Guv?' called the fat man, as I finished dressing. 'We're just brewing up.'

I had to hurry away to the surgery, where Dr Farquarson was sportingly giving me breakfast, but the temptation to sneak back at lunchtime to see what they had done was irresistible. I found the three still sitting round the fire, now eating sandwiches. I wondered if they had been there all morning, but as the room was littered with paint-pots and buckets I supposed that one of them must have stirred some time.

'We're waiting for the ladders, Guv,' explained the fat man cheerfully, his mouth full of bread and beetroot. 'They've got to send 'em on the other lorry.'

I apologized for disturbing them, and retired to tidy up my own quarters. Through the open sitting-room door I heard the thin one announce, 'Surprisin' what people will buy for 'ouses these days, ain't it?'

'Yes,' agreed the fat one. 'I can't say I think much of this job. Cor! It's as draughty as a chicken run.'

'Them windows is all wrong as well. Warped.'

'And look at them floors.'

'Well, *I* wouldn't live in it, that's straight.'

'We don't 'ave to, thank Gawd. Still, I suppose the people knows what they're about. He's a doctor, ain't he?'

'Doctors is made of money,' said the old man. 'You've only got to look at the stamps on your 'ealth card.'

They then started a brisk argument on football pools, which I hoped would occupy them until it was time to knock off work.

'They've established a bridgehead,' I told Nikki on the telephone in the evening. 'They spent today consolidating their positions, and tomorrow they might begin active operations. There's one thing, thank God – even though we have to live with this

219

trio for the first five years of our married life, Mr Doggett can't charge a penny more for it.'

I put down the instrument and was surprised to find the builder himself in the hall, looking worried and clutching his hat as though it were some sort of moral life-belt.

'Might I have a word with you, Doctor?' he asked anxiously.

'Well ... is it urgent, Mr Doggett? I'm just starting my surgery.'

He said it was, so I suggested 'Perhaps you'd like to slip into the consulting-room for a minute?'

He sat down with his hat on his knees and announced, 'I've been looking at them there soffits of yours, Doctor.'

'Soffits?' It sounded like some sort of French confectionary.

He nodded. 'They're a bit of a joke, you know,' he continued solemnly. 'They'll all have to come off.'

'Oh, really? Would it be a big job?'

'Few shillings only, Doctor. But I thought you ought to know.'

'That's perfectly all right, Mr Doggett,' I said with relief. 'Just add it to the bill. Is that all there is?'

'Yes, that's all, Doctor. Thank you very much.' He replaced his hat and left me with the prospect of a life free of soffits, whatever they were.

When I looked into Floral Cottage during my rounds the next morning, I was glad to see that the trio had at last started work. You could tell that because they were singing. I doubted if they sang purely from the joy of artistic creation as they slapped distemper on the ceiling but rather to occupy their nervous system, because they each seemed to know only one tune. The fat man repeated *You Made Me Love You*, the thin one alternated with the first four lines of *Underneath The Arches*, and the old man whistled a bit of *William Tell* as he discharged his duty of watching the kettle boil.

'I hear you're getting married, Guv,' said the fat one as I opened the front door. They now accorded me the privilege of accepting me as an equal.

'That's right.'

'I've been married eighteen years,' remarked the thin one, between strokes of his brush. 'I wouldn't if I was you.'

'Go on with you,' said the fat one. 'There's nothing like marriage. Buttons on your shirt

221

and hot dinners every Sunday.'

'And that's about all,' said his companion.

'I only hope,' I told them, 'that you'll be finished here before you see me carrying the bride over the threshold.'

'Don't you worry, Guv. There ain't all that much more to do.'

But that evening I was surprised to find Mr Doggett again in the hall. He was still clutching his hat and looking anxious.

'It's that there plumbing of yours, Doctor,' he said, when he had sat down.

'Plumbing? What about it?'

'Well... It's a bit of a joke, you know. It'll all have to come out.'

'Good God! Won't that be terribly expensive?'

'Not so much in your job, Doctor. Just a few quid, that's all.'

'If it must be done it must, I suppose. Put it on the bill.'

'Thank you, Doctor. Then there's them there fylfots of yours.'

'Fylfots!'

'They're a bit of a joke, you know. They'll all have to come out.'

'But isn't that a tremendous operation?' Fylfots sounded like something fundamental in the foundations.

'Only a few shillings, Doctor.'

'Oh, well, take them out, then.'

'Thank you, Doctor. It's a pleasure to do business with a straightforward man like yourself, if I may say so.'

The next day he appeared to tell me that the lavatory was a bit of a joke, and the one after it was the front door and something called the architraves. The following morning I was horrified to get a letter from Messrs Doggett and Buzzard respectfully requesting advance payment of seventy–five pounds in respect of work carried out at above site.

'Seventy-five pounds!' I exclaimed to Nikki on the telephone. 'Think of it! Why, the whole estimate was quids less than that. That rogue and swindler Doggett! He's been sticking it on right and left. I've a damned good mind to get Mr Robbinson to issue a writ.'

'But darling, does it matter so long as we get a nice little home of our own.'

'We'll never get a nice little home of our own. We'll get a nice little home of the Pier Attendants' Benefit Society, or whatever it is. And at this rate we won't even have enough left to buy a frying-pan and a tin-opener as well. You wait,' I added, banging the phone book with my fist. 'Just wait till I see that Doggett fellow again.'

'Don't be too angry with him, dear. He seemed such a nice man.'

'Angry with him? I'll shake the blighter to his very soffits!'

I summoned Mr Doggett to see me at the surgery that evening. He sat in the patient's chair looking more miserable than usual.

'Of course, all them items mount up,' he admitted, gripping his hat.

'Mount up! I'll say they do! Why, at this rate we don't need a house at all – we can spend our entire married life at the Savoy for about half the price.'

He hung his head. 'I'm sorry, Doctor.'

'If you think I'm going to hand over seventy-five pounds just like that, Mr Doggett, you're damned well mistaken. I'm going into this matter. I'm going over your work with a magnifying glass. I'm going to get my solicitor in London–'

To my alarm, two large tears spilled from Mr Doggett's eyes down his cheeks.

'Don't be too hard on me, Doctor,' he sobbed.

'But my dear Mr Doggett, I'm so sorry. I'd no idea I'd–'

'Times are very bad with me.' He wiped

his eyes lavishly on his sleeve. 'I dunno, Doctor. Once I was full of vim and go, but now I feel that miserable I don't know where to turn. I can't sleep and I can't eat proper. Sometimes I wish I wasn't here at all. I can't even have a pint to cheer myself up because of this here pain in my stomach.'

'Pain?' I looked interested. 'How long have you had it?'

'A year, on and off. I'm not signed on with any doctor, you see.'

I looked at him earnestly. 'As you're here, perhaps you'd better lie down on the couch and slip off your things,' I suggested. 'Do you get the pain before or after food? And is there any sickness?'

'Of all the builders in Hampden Cross we had to pick the neurotic one,' I told Nikki when she came up the next day. 'Why, the poor chap's a melancholic. And he's got a functional dyspepsia, or even a duodenal ulcer, into the bargain. Damn it! I ought to have spotted it when I first set eyes on him.'

'What did you do, dear?'

'What could I do? I couldn't just say, "It's a bit of a joke you know, it'll all have to come out". I took him on as a patient.'

'And you paid his bill?'

'Good lord, yes. Remember the first object

of treatment is to remove the source of the patient's anxiety.' I looked down at the sheet of paper I held. 'Though I must say, Nikki, it's rather knocked my careful budgeting for six. Can't we cut down a bit on the furniture? Do we really need three chairs in the house?'

'Darling, do be sensible. Supposing somebody calls?'

'We could borrow old Farquy's shooting-stick, or something.'

'Richard, you really must take this seriously. And don't forget you're coming round the furniture shops with me on Thursday.'

'Oh, dear! Must I?'

'Richard! Remember, you promised.'

'Oh, all right, Nikki.'

'After all, darling, it's only a fortnight till the wedding. And we must have some furniture of some sort.'

'I see your point,' I said. 'Though I must admit, there's a hell of a lot to be said for the Arabian idea of sitting on the floor and eating with your fingers.'

18

It was either the stimulating effect of my treatment or the stimulating effect of my seventy-five pounds, but Mr Doggett managed to finish at Floral Cottage in another couple of days. The three men retreated from room to room, taking their fire and teapot with them, until they made their final brew out in the back garden. As I paid the bill I reflected that the laughter of beautiful women was cheaper to enjoy these days than the honest ring of hammer on chisel. Nikki meanwhile seemed to be insisting that all manner of utensils and oddments were essential to our married life. I started having dreams in which I found myself chased by furious ironmongers or struggling with gangs of builders in bowler hats trying to brick me into the ramparts of the Tower of London. I assumed that this was a manifestation of the normal psychological disturbance before marriage.

Then there was another complication.

'I've got a proper surprise for you,' said

Kitten Strudwick after surgery one evening.

She opened the waiting-room door and led in a pale young man with spectacles and a blue suit, whom I recognized as a gas-fitting salesman I had just treated for varicose veins.

'This is Harold,' she explained. 'We're going to get married.'

'Good Lord, are you!' I exclaimed. The idea of Kitten's emotional life extending much further than the Palais and the Odeon came as a shock. 'I mean, how wonderful. It certainly seems a catching complaint, doesn't it? My heartiest congratulations,' I said, shaking hands with Harold. 'And long life and happiness to you both.'

'Thank you, Doctor,' replied Harold solemnly. 'I might add, had it not been for your good self Catherine and I would not thus have been blissfully brought together.'

'We met in the waiting-room,' Kitten explained. 'The day you were such a long time over Mrs Derridge's sinuses.'

'Might I now intrude further on your valuable time, Doctor?' Harold continued, as I motioned them to seats. 'I have long believed, Doctor, that all persons about to be joined in the state of holy matrimony should first undergo an extensive physical examination.'

'Well ... perhaps that's putting it a bit seriously. As far as I'm concerned, I think doctors should be kept out of it as much as possible. I'd say if you feel strong enough to walk up the aisle you're all right.'

'I also believe that the happy couple should have a frank talk with their doctor before the ceremony.'

I put my fingertips together as I caught Kitten's eye. 'Er ... yes, I suppose you're right.'

'Sex,' Harold continued, as though describing some particularly attractive form of gas-fitting, 'is, as they say, an important factor in marriage.'

I agreed, though I felt at the moment that it took second place to Doggett & Buzzard in ours.

'I should like now, Doctor,' Harold went on, warming a little, 'for you to give my future wife and myself a frank talk.'

He folded his arms expectantly. I noticed Kitten was grinning broadly over his shoulder, and I shifted in the surgery chair. I had many times since qualification been asked to give patients several years my senior frank talks on their sex lives. I always felt that I discharged this professional duty inadequately, because the St Swithin's teaching staff had a sound British attitude to such things and any patient mentioning sex was immediately packed off to the psychiatrists. I felt that Kitten knew far more about the subject than I did, and I was sure she was anxious to hear my views on her future sex life only for the light it would throw on my own.

'Well, you see,' I said, starting at the beginning, 'in marriage there's a man ... and a woman ... and possibly children.'

'I am naturally concerned about our relations, Doctor.'

'Oh, I shouldn't think they'd mind if you had children a bit.'

'I mean our sexual relations.'

'Quite, of course. Well, now. There are several excellent books on the subject, you know.' Grimsdyke had once recommended one to a married couple, and the man had angrily reappeared the next day having fallen out of bed and fractured his ankle. 'But most people worry too much about the whole business,' I continued. 'That's how you get a neurosis. After all, sex is nothing to get excited about. I mean, it doesn't do to... When are you getting married?' I asked

Kitten abruptly, feeling that the consultation was being held under too many difficulties to be effective.

'Next May. But I want to leave next week, please.'

'So soon?'

'Harold has to go back to Hartlepool.'

'Of course you may leave when you wish, Miss Strudwick. Though we shall all be sorry to lose you.'

'I've quite liked it here. Life's interesting.'

'And I am sure you'll find life with Harold here even more so. I suppose I'd better advertise for a new receptionist in this week's paper. Good evening, now, to you both. I hope you'll be very happy. If you want to know any more, why not go and see the Vicar?'

I hoped that had set them up physiologically for life.

'It's a nuisance about the lass leaving,' said Dr Farquarson when I told him. 'Particularly when you're so preoccupied with impending matrimony yourself.'

'I could stay here and work all next Thursday,' I said eagerly. 'Nikki only wants me to meet her to do some shopping in Town.'

'Och, I wouldn't hear of it for a moment, Richard. Anyway, the work's slackening off a

231

bit. There's nothing like a few fine days in midwinter for making folk forget how ill they are. And anyway, getting married's a much tougher job than running a practice.'

I agreed with him. At that stage the preparations for our marriage seemed to be as complicated as Noah's preparations for the Flood.

I left Floral Cottage early on the Thursday and met Nikki outside a large furniture store in Oxford Street.

'We'll choose the curtains first, darling,' said Nikki. 'I won't get anything you don't like every bit as much as I do.'

'Fine! You won't forget our little budget, though, will you dear?'

'We only want some cheap contemporary designs. Just something to keep us out of sight of the neighbours.'

We were approached inside the door by a tall, silver-haired man with the lofty bearing and formal outfit of a nineteenth-century Harley Street physician.

'We want curtains,' Nikki told him, instinctively taking charge. 'Then kitchen equipment and tableware, and after that in-expensive suites and beds and bedding.' For a second I caught in his eye the expression of the wolf welcoming little Red Riding Hood.

Then he bowed low, and we followed him through thickets of Chippendale into the shop.

'This is *absolutely* contemporary,' said the young man with the high voice and the long vowel sounds in the curtain department, 'but rather busy, wouldn't you say?'

'Yes,' Nikki admitted. 'Rather busy.'

'This,' he continued, holding up another length, 'is less busy, but of course more pricey.'

'I *do* rather like that one.'

'How about that?' I interrupted, pointing to some material in the corner. 'The one with the beer-mug pattern. Rather jolly, I think. I expect you sell a lot of that?'

'Only to public houses, sir.'

'Oh.'

'And now perhaps madam would like to see an amusing little damask?'

Shortly after we had bought the pricey curtains I realized that the shopping expedition was really nothing but a conspiracy between Nikki and the salesmen. We left the curtain department ten pounds above our budget, in the kitchen department we overspent forty with ease, and there was a difference of fifty guineas between the store's notion of inexpensive suites and ours.

'I suppose we'll *have* to take this one,' I told Nikki, as we self-consciously bounced together on a double bed. 'Even though it does cost twice as much as I allowed. I really don't know how we'll ever pay all the deposits, let alone the instalments. Do you really need as many pots and pans as that? When I lived in a flatlet I found a frying-pan and an old mess-tin quite enough for anything.'

'But darling, do be reasonable! You'd soon complain if your bacon and eggs tasted of Irish stew. Assuming, of course,' she added, 'that I learn how to cook Irish stew.'

'Anyway, thank God this is the last port of call. Now we can go and have a drink. I've been dreaming about a beer for the last half-hour.'

'But Richard, you can't just go wandering into pubs. We've got to go to glass and china and linen and blankets yet. Then we must simply rush back to Richmond. I promised we'd be there at lunch-time to settle the invitations.'

'Invitations? But they all went out weeks ago.' I remembered the bitter evening when aunts and uncles were sacrificed ruthlessly as we tried to cut the list to a realistic length.

'Yes, but a lot can't come and there's lots

of people we really must ask that we'd forgotten, and there are people who've sent presents who haven't been asked, and so we must do something about it. Then we've got to settle about the reception and fix the photographer and you'll have to meet the bridesmaids. By the way, what presents will you be buying them?'

'A packet of Player's apiece, at this rate.'

'I think they'd like ear-rings, Richard, and that's the traditional gift. Right, we'll have this,' Nikki told the salesman. 'Now how about hanging cupboards?'

In Nikki's home, the table in the sitting-room where I had first been received looked like a shoplifter's den after an energetic but erratic day. All round, the chairs were draped with dresses and the floor was deep in hatboxes, and a number of young women were chattering excitedly amid the disorder like birds after a hurricane.

'This is Jane,' said Nikki. 'And this is Cissy, and this is Helen, and this is Carmen, and this is Greta.'

She introduced five girls, all of whom looked to me the same. They stared at me for some seconds with uninhibited curiosity before returning to trying on hats.

'Now,' said Nikki, 'we must decide

whether the invitation that Mummy's old nanny refused can go to Lady Horridge, because a title would look good in the account in the local paper, or to Mrs Grisewood who was so nice to Mummy and Daddy when they were in Madeira. By the way, it's only sandwiches for lunch. I'm afraid. And I'd kept a bottle of beer for you, but Robin seems to have drunk it.'

Thenceforward no one seemed to take much notice of me, though Aunt Jane got me in a corner and said she thought we were very, very brave getting married at all in such difficult times. I agreed with her. Later, Robin arrived with his father from the City, and after pointing out that several presents were well known to fall to pieces immediately on use, asked 'Where are you going for the honeymoon?'

'South of France.'

'What, at this time of the year? Didn't you know the rainfall comes in February? And it's the worst season they've had for years down there, too. I met a chap today in the City who's only just come back.'

'Thank you,' I said. 'On the strength of your kind advice I shall cancel the bookings, and Nikki and I will go to Manchester instead.'

'Manchester? That's rather an odd place for a honeymoon, isn't it?'

Fortunately the Commander spotted me, and carried me off to his cubby-hole for a gin.

I had been invited to stay the night, but as two of the bridesmaids were also in the house I had to share a room with Robin, who not only snored but got up at six and did exercises. I left alone early the next morning, because I had my own shopping to do. First I went to the travel agent for the tickets, then to the jewellers to collect the wedding-ring, then to fix the flowers and confirm the cars, afterwards to buy the bridesmaids' earrings, and finally to try on my own clothes. It is a curious reflection on the psychology of the British middle-classes that their inhibitions about appearing un-suitably dressed for any occasion overcome their inhibitions about getting into a pair of trousers already favoured by half a dozen unknown occupants. As I was expected to be married in the costume of a Young Man About Town at the start of the century, like every other male on the invitation list I went to a large clothes shop near Regent Street where they could fit you out by the day for anything from a hunt to the House of Lords.

'Yes, sir?' said one of the aristocratic-looking figures inside the door as I nervously approached.

'I wanted to ... er, that is...' I felt like the first time I took my microscope to the pawnbroker's. 'I wondered if it would be possible to see someone about ... actually, the loan of some morning clothes?'

'Our hiring department would be delighted to be at your disposal, sir. Small door off the street, just round the corner.'

As I was greeted by another man inside the discreet door, the performance suddenly brought a sense of *déjà vu*, as though I had somehow observed it all before. The first nervous and shameful enquiry, the cheerfully broadminded tone of the directions, the sheltered door, the tactful segregation, the air of silent comradeship among the other customers... Of course! I had it. The VD Department at St Swithin's.

'Would you take the end one, sir?' asked the attendant, my morale rising rapidly as I walked down the line of cubicles overhearing 'Yes, My Lord ... of course, General ... not at all, Professor ... the trousers are perhaps a shade too tight, Your Grace?'

'We'll fix you up in a jiffy, Doctor,' he continued, looking at me with the glance of an experienced undertaker. 'How about a lilac waistcoat? Just the thing for a wedding.'

I took the lilac waistcoat, and also a grey top hat specially cased in a black tin box resembling those used by pathologists for taking interesting organs back to their laboratories. As I stowed my trousseau in the back of the car before driving off for a weekend's duty in Hampden Cross, it suddenly occurred to me that in eight days' time Nikki and I would be man and wife.

19

'My heavens, darling! You can't possibly wear that!' said Nikki in horror. After another week of fevered preparation we had reached the day before the wedding. I had just shown her the lilac waistcoat.

'But why ever not?' I felt hurt. 'I rather like it. And the man said it would give a festive air to what I always thought was a festive occasion.'

'But I positively refuse to be seen in church or anywhere else with you wearing that.'

'It's a jolly nice waistcoat,' I said more warmly. 'And after all, I don't make nasty comments about your wedding-dress.'

'I didn't make a nasty comment, Richard. I merely expressed a reasonable opinion.'

'Oh, all right, all right! I'll take it back and change it when we get to Town this afternoon.'

'You can't this afternoon – the Vicar might want us for a rehearsal.'

'Must we really have one? We've only got a

240

couple of lines of dialogue in the whole performance.'

'We've got to choose the music. I told the Vicar I wanted to make my entry to the *Trumpet Voluntary*.'

'What's wrong with old Mendelssohn's *Wedding March?* Everyone else has it.'

'That's the point, Richard. Everyone does.'

'Oh, have anything you like,' I grumbled. 'Have *The Entry of the Gladiators* if you want to.'

'Richard! You don't seem at all interested in your own wedding.'

'I hardly look on it as my wedding. It seems to be only yours.'

'Richard!'

Suddenly she came close to me.

'We mustn't have a row, darling,' she whispered. 'Not just before we're married.'

'Of course not, my sweet. Let's keep them all until just after.'

We laughed, and I kissed her until I heard Dr Farquarson's footsteps outside the surgery.

'I've got to go away and see two or three cases before we can get to London,' I told her. 'I'll meet you back here for a cup of tea, then we'll be off.'

241

'I'll go down to the cottage, darling. Just to see if everything's all right.'

It is understandable that I didn't give my patients my most powerful attention that afternoon. I made flashing diagnoses and scribbled my prescriptions, and I was back in the surgery within half an hour.

'There's a lady wot's waiting for you inside,' announced the old woman who cleaned our front steps and our brass plate.

'Damn it! A patient?'

'No, she says she's come for that there receptionist's job.'

'I'd clean forgotten I'd got to fix that.' The advertisement had appeared in that week's paper, but was apparently less inviting than Grimsdyke's charm. 'As she's the only applicant, I might as well let her have the job on the spot if she's respectable.'

Waiting in the surgery was Sally Nightingale from St Swithin's.

'Good God!' I cried. 'You!'

'Surprised?' she said, with a laugh.

'Surprised? Demoralized!' I took a good look at her. 'But what on earth are you doing here?'

'I only live in Barnet.'

'I mean in this surgery.'

'I have come in answer to your advertisement, as the expression is.'

'You mean, you really want the job?'

She nodded. 'My nursing career having been brought to an abrupt, end, I tried the stage. Repertory, you know, up north. *Othello* sandwiched between *Charley's Aunt* and *Where The Rainbow Ends*. But alas! Despite an enviable self-confidence, I soon found I wasn't as good at acting as I was at nursing. And it was harder on the feet. Then there was a horrible stage-manager who tried to seduce me one night in the interval. When I was playing Hamlet's mother, too. I used that as an excuse to walk out and abandon the profession for good. So here I am, looking for gainful employment.' She sat herself on the desk and swung her legs.

'But what about Godfrey?' I exclaimed.

'Godfrey?'

'John Godfrey. That pilot fellow you ran off with from St Swithin's.'

'Richard, dear, what in heaven's name are you talking about?'

'Roger Hinxman told me you'd eloped with him to South America. Hence your abrupt departure.'

She laughed. 'Roger *is* an old fool, really. I'm sorry I walked out on you both. But it was due to circumstances beyond my control.' Seeing my expression, she explained, 'I was chucked out.'

'Chucked out?'

'My second-year report came up, and within ten minutes I was summoned to matron's office and told politely that continuing my training would be a waste of time all round. To spare my feelings I was allowed to slip away and nothing official was said about it. Hence the mystery, I suppose.'

'But what on earth did they chuck you out for, Sally? You were such a good nurse.'

'It was silly, really. But you know what matrons are. They said I got too friendly with the patients.'

'But how stupid! Why...' Suddenly I paused. 'You mean, that ridiculous business with Hinxman and myself had something to do with it?'

'I suppose it did, in a way,' she admitted. 'It had got to Matron's ears, anyway. But it was all my fault. Now,' she said, with determined cheerfulness. 'How about the job?'

This put me in as delicate a position as any man since Solomon. There was no doubt, I felt remorsefully, that my behaviour in Sally's ward had ended her nursing career.

But can a bridegroom start employing his old flames the night before his wedding, however well they are extinguished? I realized now the sense of Sally's remark that convalescent patients should never meet their nurses over the dinner-table. She was a pleasant enough person, certainly, but seen without uniform and from levels above the horizontal she looked like a jolly schoolgirl out for the half-hols.

'Well,' I said guardedly, deciding to say nothing about my own status for the moment. 'You may find this sort of job rather difficult.'

'But it's just my cup of tea! It's absolutely made for an unfrocked nurse.'

'Yes, but...'

'Seriously, Richard, I *should* like it, if you'll have me. It's near home and it'll give me the evenings free to go and help look after mother. It'll be wonderful dealing with patients again, and you can't imagine what it means to work with someone you know after being in that beastly rep.'

What could I say?

'All right,' I told her. 'You can start on Monday.'

'Richard! You dear. I feel I want to kiss you.'

'No, no, please! I mean – not ... not... You see, Sally, I must explain that many things have happened–'

'Oh, don't worry, Richard,' she laughed. 'But just six months ago you *did* love me to distraction and told poor Roger you wanted to marry me, didn't you?'

'I suppose I did,' I confessed.

'I was really quite fond of you, too. But from painful experience I knew it wouldn't last once your temperature was down.'

'Perhaps,' I said anxiously, 'you might develop amnesia about the little affair?'

'I promise. But it's really quite fascinating in retrospect. Your partner thought so, anyway. I said I knew you personally when I arrived, and before I knew where I was I'd told the whole story, proposals and all.'

'To Dr Farquarson, you mean?'

'Is that her name? The nice young lady doctor who was here when I came.'

'I believe you met the girl who came to apply for the receptionist's job?' I asked Nikki.

It was half an hour later. I had loaded my cases into the car, and for the last time we were starting off to London. Nikki's manner since returning from the cottage was as

246

remote as the far side of the moon, and just as cold.

'Yes. I did.'

I pressed the starter. 'She's Florence Nightingale.'

'Really, Richard! I–'

'That actually is her name. Didn't I tell you I knew her at St Swithin's?'

'You overlooked it.'

'Did I? Funny how I forgot.'

'It also slipped your memory that you proposed to her about a month before you did to me.'

'Nikki, as it happens, I can easily explain that.'

'Please do.'

'You see, I was slightly unbalanced at the time. I was having jaundice, remember. You know you get mental changes, don't you?'

'I'm wondering whether they're permanent.'

I edged my way into the London Road traffic.

'I suppose you've given her the job?' Nikki asked.

'As a matter of fact,' I said, staring intently at the tailboard of the lorry in front, 'I have.'

Nikki said nothing.

'You see, darling,' I went on quickly,

247

'everything was over and done with long ago between Sally Nightingale and me. Well, six months ago, anyway. But I *did* feel I had a sort of debt to her, because it was through me that she got chucked out of the hospital. I mean,' I added, feeling that I was not putting my case at its strongest, 'it will be so nice for her to be able to get home to her old mother in the evenings.'

Nikki still said nothing.

'You *do* understand, darling, don't you?'

'Oh, perfectly, Richard. As you say, it'll be nice for her mother.'

'Good,' I said, most uneasily.

We crawled along the road for about half a mile without exchanging a word. Thinking I had better restart the conversation as we drew up at the traffic lights, I said 'I suppose we'd better make up our minds about the music we want at the wedding.'

In a pointedly normal voice Nikki said 'I suppose we must.'

'Do you still want the *Trumpet Voluntary?*'

'I can't really see anything wrong with it.'

'It's a very fine piece of music,' I agreed. 'But so is Mendelssohn's *Wedding March*.'

'The *Wedding March* is about the most hackneyed tune in the world. It booms from practically every organ in Britain on a

248

Saturday afternoon.'

'But so does the *Trumpet Voluntary*. It's what they use at Harringay to get the boxers into the ring.'

'Richard! There's no need to be insulting.'

'I'm not being insulting. I'm being perfectly reasonable about the serious question of church music.'

'You're not. You're being damned annoying and pigheaded. You haven't been a bit helpful in getting ready for the wedding–'

'A bit helpful! I like that! First of all you've ruined me with your outrageous extravagance–'

'Extravagance! Do you know what it's like to furnish a house on the never-never?'

'I haven't been able to do any work because I'm always being dragged round some shop or other in London–'

'I suppose you expect me to get a home together entirely by myself?'

'No, but I think we could have done with a flat instead.'

'You do, do you? If you'd married your other girl friend–'

'She's not my girl friend!'

'Whom you are now installing comfortably in your surgery–'

'I tell you I was sorry for her mother!'

'If you're so idiotic as to expect me to take that as an excuse for playing fast and loose–'

'I am *not* playing fast and loose! The girl means nothing to me whatever. Anyway, what about you and Grimsdyke?'

'Me and Grimsdyke? What on earth do you mean?'

'The way you were carrying on with him that night in the Bull.'

'Richard! I've never heard such beastly rubbish in all my–'

We were interrupted by a fanfare of car horns as the lights changed to green.

'Oh!' cried Nikki. 'You're impossible!' She pulled her glove off. 'There's your ring back. Goodbye!'

She leapt out of the car and slammed the door. I drove steadfastly on to London.

20

Grimsdyke had taken a small flat in a large block in Chelsea. I left the car outside, stamped into the lift, and banged on his door.

'Here comes the bride,' he greeted me brightly. 'All ready for the big day, old boy? Which side are you going to hold your orange blossom?'

'There's not going to be any wedding,' I told him. I flung Nikki's ring on the table. 'It's off.'

'Off! But whatever for?'

'We had a row.'

'Good Lord! What about?'

'The music we were going to have in church.'

'The ... the what, old lad?'

'I told you – the music. She wanted the *Trumpet Voluntary*. I wanted the *Wedding March*. We had a disagreement about it, and now the wedding's off.'

'Richard, old man,' he said anxiously. 'I always thought you were a bit balmy, but I didn't know you were quite so cracked as that.'

'Well, you know how these things are. It was like your blasted draughts game at Foulness. One thing led to another. Old scores were raked up. Before I knew where I was, I'd got a spare ring on my hands.'

'You need a drink,' said Grimsdyke.

'I do,' I said.

'But you can't put the wedding off now, old lad,' he complained, pouring me half a tumbler of whisky. 'I've laid on a tremendous bachelor party for you tonight. Tony Benskin and all the boys are coming. Even old uncle Farquarson's appearing, determined to add his Edinburgh repertoire to our usual songs, God help us.'

'You'll just have to ring up and put them all off. I'll have to wire all the wedding guests, anyway.'

'But Richard, you chump! Can't you be sensible?'

'I am being sensible! Perfectly cool, calm, and sensible. It's perfectly obvious that Nikki and I–'

'But you can't behave like this!'

'Now at last I can behave as I damn well like.'

The doorbell rang.

'Oh, damn!' said Grimsdyke. He admitted Tony Benskin, who was looking much the same as when suffering incipient fatherhood in St Swithin's.

'You're a bit soon for the party, Tony,' said Grimsdyke shortly. 'Did Molly let you off the chain early or something?'

'Is that a drink?' demanded Benskin. He grabbed my glass, murmured 'Hello, Richard,' and took a long swig. 'There isn't a chain any more, Grim,' he announced. 'Molly and I have separated.'

'What!' we cried together.

'Irrevocably and completely separated,' said Benskin, swallowing the rest of the whisky. 'Molly's gone back to mother. She went this afternoon, taking young Tristram.'

'But why on earth?' exclaimed Grimsdyke.

'Why? Hah! I've never known a woman to behave in such a ridiculous, unappreciative, and generally dangerous manner.'

'But what did she do, Tony?' he asked. 'Pull a gun on you, or something?'

'Oh, it's not me. It's what she's been doing to poor little Tristram. Do you know, I've bought pretty well every book on infant feeding and child welfare there is, and Molly absolutely and completely refuses to do what I tell her. Do you realize, when every

253

single authority says you've got to start a baby on a cup at six months, she insists on keeping him on the bottle? Think what she's doing to the poor little thing's psychology! He might develop all sorts of frightful unpleasant habits when he grows up. She says the bottle's easier and he likes it, so there.' Benskin poured himself another drink, 'Then there's the matter of putting him out in his pram. Of course you put children out in their prams, even if it's bloody well freezing. Stimulates the metabolism no end. But Molly says his feet get cold. Oh, and lots of things besides. Vitamins and immunization and conditioned potting and God knows what. She accused me of interfering. I accused her of ignorance. We had a hell of a row over lunch, and she walked out.'

'You're not the only one,' Grimsdyke told him morosely. 'Richard's nuptials are off, too.'

'And a jolly good thing,' said Benskin warmly. 'Never, never, never get married, old boy! Stick to the single life while you've got a chance.'

'What rubbish,' said Grimsdyke. 'Now look here, you idiots. I know you've always regarded me as the licensed lady-killer of our little band, but I don't mind telling you that you're both damned lucky because you've got yourselves attached to a couple of wonderful girls who are about fifty times too good for your miserable characters anyway. Richard, you can get into your car and go crawling back to Nikki and crave forgiveness and ask her to wipe her feet on your neck.'

'Never!'

'That's right, old boy,' Benskin told me. 'You stick up for yourself. Let the ruddy woman go and stew in her own juice.'

'If you do, Richard,' said Grimsdyke, 'you'll end up a repulsive old bachelor with tender memories. And a fat lot of good tender memories are for keeping your feet warm in bed.'

'What the hell can you know about it, anyway?' I said angrily. 'You've never been married.'

'The spectator sees more of the game, doesn't he?'

For a second we stared each other in the eye, then I collapsed on Grimsdyke's divan and said 'This is absolutely ridiculous. Six months ago Tony was telling me how wonderful it was to get married, and you were telling me not to touch a wedding-ring with a barge-pole. And now here's Tony congratulating me on my lucky escape and you're telling me I'm committing moral suicide.'

'Well, damn it,' said Grimsdyke. 'I've got more sense than either of you fellows. I've never got myself in a mess like this to start with.'

The argument continued. Tony refused to go back to Molly. I refused to grovel to Nikki. Grimsdyke finally refused to have anything to do with either of us. We were interrupted only by another ring on the doorbell and the appearance of Dr Farquarson.

'I thought I'd arrived rather early for the party,' he said to Grimsdyke, putting down his hat among the glasses. 'But I see it's already begun.'

The three of us said nothing. We were all staring in different directions, trying to look as though we'd been having a jolly time.

'But still, now I'm here I'll take a dram.' We stood in silence, while Grimsdyke hastily poured his uncle a drink. 'I don't think I've had the pleasure of meeting your other friend?'

'That is Tony Benskin, uncle,' Grimsdyke muttered. 'Tony, Dr Farquarson.'

Tony Benskin nodded absently.

'Well now, you young fellows. I'm a bit of an old fogy, but I still flatter myself I can rise to the occasion when required. We should have a high old time tonight and no mistake, eh? After all, it's the happiest of occasions. A young man getting married. Who could argue with that?'

'Oh, quite.' I stuffed my hands into my trouser pockets.

'Your very good health, Richard my boy.' Dr Farquarson raised his glass. 'On this most joyful occasion.' He looked round at us. 'Aren't you young fellows drinking at all?'

We hastily found glasses and gave the toast, with the enthusiasm and the expressions of men honouring a suicide pact.

'On the whole,' said Dr Farquarson, filling his pipe. 'I'm in favour of weddings. If a couple can survive the emotional strain, hard work, and demands for tact and self-discipline they involve, they can overcome pretty well anything else in their married life to come.'

I said nothing.

'Marriage,' Dr Farquarson continued, 'is a strange psychological cat's-cradle. And as you know, it's generally easier to make a cat's-cradle if you don't worry yourself stiff whether it's going to collapse before you've started. Och, I'm not saying that every main road in the country should be signposted to Gretna Green. But it's a good idea to take the complications of modern marriage in your stride, like you take the complications of modern motoring. Try and reduce it to its simplest essentials. It's just another example of my favourite theory about civilization being too much for us. Any of you fellows got a match?'

The three of us offered him matchboxes.

'Hello,' he said, picking up Nikki's ring from the table. 'Haven't I seen this somewhere before?'

'Yes,' I said quickly. 'But it wasn't fitting very well, so Nikki gave it to me to take down to the jewellers and get it altered.'

'I see. What was I rambling on about now? I remember. But fortunately, marriage is about the only thing left in our lives that can be reduced to its essentials by the thought of a moment. You just have to ask, Do I love the girl? Then you have to ask, Does she love me? Page one, chapter one, any biology textbook. If the answer's 'yes' in both cases, you needn't worry about incompatibility of temperament and whether you like your eggs boiled or scrambled.'

I wished heartily that Dr Farquarson would finish his drink and get out.

'Or even,' he continued, 'who you give the job of receptionist to.'

For the first time I noticed his eyebrows quivering.

'Dr Farquarson–!'

'The young lady of yours is in my car,' he said. 'I met her in the surgery and dried her tears and exercised an old man's privilege of talking the hind leg off a donkey.' As the bell rang, he added, 'That'll be her now. I just wanted time to say my piece, that's all.'

'Nikki darling!' I exclaimed, throwing open the door. I nearly embraced Molly Benskin and her baby.

'Tony angel!' she cried, pushing past me into the room.

'Molly, my sweet!'

'How can you forgive me, Tony? You were absolutely right about the cup and the potty and putting him out in the cold.'

'No, no, no, darling! How can you possibly forgive *me?* I was absolutely wrong about everything.'

'Tony, no!' she said, bursting into tears. 'It was all my fault. Every bit.'

As I started to rush downstairs, I heard

Grimsdyke exclaim 'I knew women made chaps a bit soft in the head, but I never quite thought I'd run into benefit night at Bedlam like this.'

'Nikki, my dearest, sweetest, little lovely one!' I said, embracing her wildly on the pavement, to the alarm of a man delivering the milk.

'Richard darling! My beautifullest loveliest little bunny-wunny!'

'How can I ask you to forgive me? How can I cringe enough? Won't you please wipe your shoes on my neck?'

'But darling, the whole thing's been my own silly stupid fault.'

'Yours? Nonsense, Nikki! I'm to blame all along. I was a ridiculous silly idiot.'

'Sweet Richard.' She ran her fingers through my hair. 'How can you want to marry such a shrew as me?'

'If you're a shrew, may you never ever be tamed.'

'I love you so much, darling one.'

'So do I. To distraction.'

'Do you two mind if I have my car back?'

We jumped apart at Dr Farquarson's voice behind us.

'I'll be seeing you later this evening, Richard my lad,' he added, opening the door. 'I'm off to Mappin and Webb's to buy a wedding present.'

'But you've already given us one, Farquy.'

'But didn't I tell you? Our Miss Wildewinde went back to old Dr Mc-Burney, and would you believe it they're getting married next week. It'll do them both a power of good. Yes, there's a lot of it about at this season, as we say to the patients when there's nothing we can do to stop it.'

21

'Rise and shine!' called Grimsdyke heartily. *'For I'm to be married today – today. Yes, I'm to be married today!'*

I sat bolt upright. 'What time is it?'

'Eleven-thirty.'

'Good God! Only another three hours and we've got to be at the church!'

'Steady on, old lad! You don't take three hours to get dressed on an ordinary day, do you?'

'But this isn't an ordinary day. God!' I tried to stand up, but stopped abruptly. 'My head! What on earth did you give me to drink last night?'

'Oh, just beer and whisky and gin and brandy and port and vodka and so on.'

I became aware of my surroundings. Grimsdyke's flat resembled a ship's cabin after a heavy gale, and I had been sleeping on the floor with my head on Dr Farquarson's hat and wearing Tony Benskin's jacket and a grass skirt.

'Where did I get this grass thing from?'

'What, the skirt? From the girl in that night-club, of course.'

'What girl in what night-club?'

'Come off it, Richard! You couldn't have been as blotto as that.'

'The last thing I can remember is when we were all thrown out of that pub. With Nikki's brother slapping me on the back and telling me I wasn't such a bad fellow after all.'

'The skirt came much later. It was the girl old Farquy kept wanting to dance with. Believe me, I've never seen the old uncle in such form since Scotland won in the last minute at Twickenham. Don't worry,' he added, 'she only gave you her spare one. You insisted it would go well in church with your lilac waistcoat.'

I groaned and laid down again. 'Have you got any codeine?'

'Better than codeine. I've got a bottle of champagne in the oven.'

'In the where?'

'As Grimsdyke doesn't indulge in home cooking, the oven's useful for hiding such stuff from a crowd of determined dypso-maniacs, such as I entertained last night. Keeps it nice and cool, too.'

I shortly afterwards had the pleasant

experience of drinking champagne in the bath.

'We've bags of time,' Grimsdyke told me. 'There's no need to worry, because you really haven't got anything more to do. It's in the enemy camp that confusion will be reigning unbounded until the Daimler with the white ribbons rolls up at the door.'

'We aren't having white ribbons,' I said firmly. 'We agreed on that long ago.'

'By the way, what music did you decide to have in the end?'

'Oh, the music,' I said lightly, as I started to shave with Grimsdyke's razor, 'I just left it to Nikki. It doesn't matter a damn.'

'I'd say it was dashed important myself, old lad,' Grimsdyke said thoughtfully. 'As she's finally decided to marry you, I should be very interested to see whether she sticks to her own *Trumpet Voluntary* or whether she bows to the wishes of her future lord and master and orders the *Wedding March*.'

'Blast!' I exclaimed. 'I've cut myself again. I'll arrive at the altar looking like Banquo's ghost.'

'If you feel anything like you look, Richard, I should think you'd be glad to find you bleed at all.'

That morning I began to realize what it

264

was like to indulge in mescalin or suffer one of the odd psychological diseases which derange your time-appreciation. At one moment time would seem to drag by like an old horse on its way to the knackers, at another it flashed past like a spaceship, and at others I felt certain it was going backwards.

'I suppose you'll think me bloody silly if I tell you not to look so worried,' Grimsdyke said to cheer me up, as I sat about in his spare dressing-gown. 'But don't forget you've only got to do it once. If Nikki discovers your true character after a couple of years and unloads you, you can marry the next one in a registry office.'

'Never again,' I said firmly. 'Never, never, never again. Do you suppose everyone feels like this?'

'Ever since Adam had his thoracotomy.'

'I wish I hadn't got this horrible vacuum sensation in my upper abdomen. I feel as if old Sir Lancelot Spratt had been at me on one of his demonstration days.'

'Have some more champers. Nothing like it for restoring the roses to the cheeks.' He looked at his watch. 'Or perhaps we'd better be getting into our finery. Then I'll pop down and get the car out.'

'Supposing it breaks down on the way?' I asked in alarm.

'Oh, it probably will. Then we'll take it in turns to push. I say, this waistcoat's pretty snappy. Did you hire it with the rest?'

'I'm glad you like it, Grim. Nikki and I had a difference of opinion about it. Do you think I ought to leave it off!'

'Leave it off! Not a bit, old lad. If you like it, wear it.'

'I'm not so sure, Grim. I really ought to do what Nikki wants.'

'Now see here, old lad. There's nothing like starting off the way you mean to go on. You wear the thing. And keep your coat open, too.'

Twenty minutes later Grimsdyke and myself stood in front of the mirror, admiring the two elegant English gentlemen before us.

'What do I do with the hat?' I asked.

'Carry it.'

'In church, I mean. They don't have cloakrooms, do they?'

'Shove it under the pew.'

'Supposing I sit on it?'

'My dear chap, don't go on making difficulties! It doesn't matter a damn what you do, anyway. Everyone will be looking at Nikki.'

'True,' I admitted.

'Well, old lad. Off to the gallows.'

'You've got the ring?' I demanded hoarsely.

'Cosy in the waistcoat pocket.'

'And you won't forget to pick up Nikki's new passport in the vestry?'

'Not on your life.'

'Oh, and the telegrams. Reading them out afterwards, I mean.'

'I shall sound like the town crier announcing tax concessions.'

'What I'm getting at is... I mean, some of the chaps from St Swithin's think themselves pretty funny at times, you know. They forget there's all sorts of sticky relatives there to hear. You'll censor them a bit, won't you, if necessary?'

'Leave it to me, Richard. I shall let no shade of embarrassment cross your rosy path today. I remember I once sent one to a girl I knew on the stage, and like a fool I tried to be topical and wrote "All the best for your first night". Husband wouldn't speak to me for months afterwards.'

'Well, that's about all, then?'

'Yes, old lad. That's about all.'

For a second we looked at each other. Grimsdyke and I had been the closest of friends since the day we had first met outside the lecture-hall at St Swithin's, when we both faced life from the laughably low status of first-year medical students. Together we had cheerfully struggled or schemed our way through the course, and together we had made our first exciting forays into the world beyond the protective walls of St Swithin's itself. Each of us knew enough comfortably to blackmail the other for life, and we would have readily shared our last crusts – provided there was absolutely no possibility of being able to swap them for half a pint of bitter. And now I was getting married, and it could never be quite the same again.

'Goodbye, Grim old man,' I said instinctively. We shook hands. 'And thanks a lot.'

'Goodbye, Richard. And all the luck. You'll need it more than me.'

'I don't know if... I mean, you're always a lot more cynical about these things than I am. I suppose you can't understand how much I really love Nikki and how wonderful all this really is to me.'

'Of course I do, old lad. All my fooling about's just to keep your knees from knocking.'

We stood clasping hands for a second, then Grimsdyke said 'The tumbril awaits' and stuck my top-hat on my head.

We were soon in the car, through the streets, at the church. I had a blurred impression of the congregation, which seemed large enough to fill the Albert Hall. There was my mother and father, there was Dr Farquarson, there was Robin stalking the aisle to ask if you were friends of the bride or bridegroom. There was the Vicar, waiting in the wings. There was the organist, twiddling idly away and glancing into his mirror like a nervous driver in a police trap.

'Don't worry, old lad,' Grimsdyke whispered in the front pew. 'Twenty minutes and it'll all be over.'

'But it ought to have started five minutes ago!' I hissed back.

'Haven't you heard the bride's always late, you idiot?'

'Perhaps she's changed her mind.'

He shook his head. 'Nikki's a sensible girl, but not as sensible as that.'

Suddenly everyone stood up.

'Here you are, Richard. On your feet.'

Glancing down the aisle I had a vision of Nikki, white and radiant at the other end. The organist stopped twiddling and struck a chord. Then he broke into Mendelssohn's *Wedding March*.

'Whacko!' said Grimsdyke delightedly, digging me in the ribs. 'She gave in in the end, old lad! From now on, you're the boss for life.'

And so we were married.

I'm sure that we shall live happily ever after. But I'm not so sure that Grimsdyke was right.

This Large Print Book, for people
who cannot read normal print,
is published under the auspices of

THE ULVERSCROFT FOUNDATION